CW01496977

NO LIMITS

CORRUPT COWBOYS

BOOK TWO

EMMA CREED

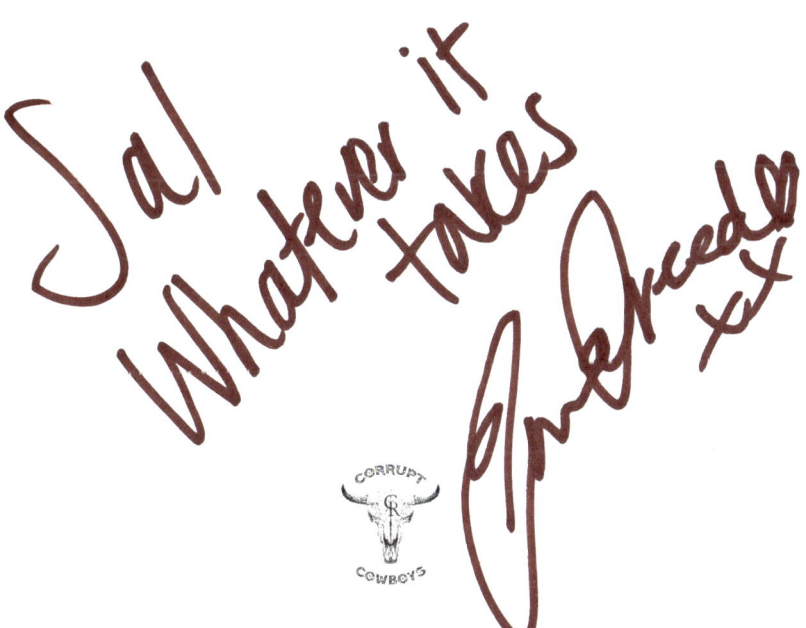

No Limits
Copyright © 2023 by Emma Creed
All rights reserved
First Edition

No part of this book may be reproduced or transmitted in any form or by any means, electronic or mechanical including photocopying, recording, or by any information storage and retrieval system without written permission of the author, except for the use of brief quotations in a book review.

This is a work of fiction. Names, characters, businesses, places, events and incidents are either the product of the author's imagination or used in a fictitious manner. Any resemblance to actual persons, living or dead, actual events, or locales is entirely coincidental. The use of any real company and/or product names is for literary effect only. All other trademarks and copyrights are the property of their respective owners.

AUTHOR NOTE

Warning

No Limits and all books in the Corrupt Cowboys series are a work of fiction and contain adult content. Due to the nature of the series you should expect come across various subject matter that some readers may find disturbing, and it is intended for readers 18+

Please contact the author if you have any questions.

WHATEVER IT TAKES

"So, what do you think of the view?" Kieron steps up behind me and rests his hands on my shoulders. The way he squeezes doesn't bring me comfort like it's supposed to. It makes me shiver.

"It's pretty." I turn my head so I can look at him, and I wonder what the hell's wrong with me. Kieron's handsome, he's funny, he's kind, and we've got so much in common.

"Pretty enough to paint, huh?" he laughs, before he presses his lips onto mine and when he tries to turn it into something more intense, I smile and pull away.

"So, did you put a deposit down?" I try to ignore the disappointed look on his face. I've gotten used to that look. If I'm being honest with myself, I'm surprised he's still trying. We've been dating for over a month, and we're still yet to get past first base.

"Yeah, it's all mine. Ours, if you want it to be?" I notice how that disappointed look has turned into a hopeful one.

"Hear me out. I know it's crazy, and we've only been dating a month, but I've been in love with you since the first day you walked into the gallery."

"Kieron...I..."

"Just think about it," he interrupts, before I can come up

with a lame-ass excuse, and suddenly I find myself feeling bad for even being here.

I'm not in love with Kieron. I should never have pretended to him, or myself, that there's ever a chance I could be.

The truth is, three years ago, Garrett Carson ruined my life. I opened my heart to him. I allowed what I thought we had to develop into something I wanted so desperately, that I got completely blindsided from reality and, ever since, I've found it impossible to desire anyone else. I must be the only twenty-one-year old virgin in L.A. It's pathetic, and it's all because there is no other man that measures up to that arrogant asshole who broke my heart.

I've tried. God, I've tried. Kieron's not the first guy I've dated. I've spent the past thirty-nine months, two weeks and four days trying to get over Garrett and trying to forget the summer that I fell in love with him, but I'm still no closer today than I was the day I left Fork River.

"I'll think about it." I fake him a smile, knowing that I'm lying to him and feeling pretty fucking rotten for it.

"So, since we're alone, with no roommates to disturb us..." Kieron's eyes glance toward the bedroom door, and nerves knot together in the pit of my stomach.

"Sure." I nod bravely, taking his hand in mine and hoping it will stop shaking as I lead him through to the bedroom. I don't look back to see if he's smiling. I just focus on what I'm gonna do.

On what I have to do.

Garrett Carson is no longer gonna be my curse. I don't care how wrong it's gonna feel. Once it's done, I'll feel better. Or at least, that's what I'm telling myself. Because I figure nothing can be worse than feeling owned by a man who doesn't want you.

I step into the room and look at the bed. It's made up with crisp, white sheets and looks almost clinical. The lighting in here's far too bright, so I turn on the lamp beside the bed and then move back toward the door to flick off the main light switch.

Kieron grabs at my waist and pulls me close, his lips invading mine again, as his hand slides up my back and starts to unzip my dress. I squeeze my eyes tighter when a vision comes into my mind. Kieron's lips feel nothing like Garrett's did. Even when we kissed through a storm, his were all I could feel. When Garrett kissed me, he consumed me, and now, here, in this apartment over a thousand miles away, it still feels like he's consuming me now. I fight against the will to stop, wrapping my arms around Kieron's neck and kissing him harder. It doesn't matter how many times I've tried, it never gets easier. But this time, I *will* persevere. I'll get through it because I like Kieron. He's a good person, he's patient, and I believe he truly wants to make me happy. I'm the only person preventing that from happening.

Kieron redirects our bodies and lays me down on the mattress, and when I open my eyes and look up at him, I feel the tears start to build in my eyes. It shouldn't be him, and it shouldn't be like this. There's no fire inside me, no tingle on my skin. My body isn't screaming for him. It's screaming for me to stop.

"I'd take my time and make sure your first experience was something you'd never forget. I'd worship your body the way it deserves, and I'd make you cum so hard, that you'd never wanna be taken by anybody else."

I hear Garrett's low, growly voice whisper in my ear like a curse, and when I close my eyes again, it's his dark, harsh stare I see judging me.

"I don't belong to you," I speak silently back to him, as

Kieron's hand travels under my dress and his fingers stretch over my body.

"You're beautiful," Kieron whispers, and the kisses he puts on my neck feel cold. My body tenses, my stomach knots and I try so hard to get past the urge to push him away.

"I'm a virgin!" I blurt the words out like they're my only defense. It's the kinda thing a guy should know before he fucks a girl, right?

Kieron pulls away, and when I look up, I see the startled look on his face.

"Are you kidding?" He smiles, and slowly I shake my head back at him.

"I can make it special." He gets back to kissing my skin, and his touch feels more like an infestation than something that's supposed to bring me pleasure.

Find someone special, who's worthy of it, but don't ever think that I won't be here wishin' it was me."

I hear that damn voice in my head again, and I dig my nails into the palms of my hands to stop myself from pushing Kieron away.

"Maisie." I'm not sure which one of them is saying my name now, but when I open my eyes and see Kieron staring back at me with those kind, patient blue eyes, I breathe out a long, heavy sigh.

"I'm sorry," I whisper, somehow managing to slide out from beneath him. I pull down the skirt part of my dress and reach behind me, trying to catch my zip as I rush back out to the living room to grab my purse and jacket.

"Maisie, wait!" Kieron chases after me, and I grab my denim jacket off the back of the couch and clutch my purse in my hands.

"It's fine, we can just talk. You don't have to leave."

"I need to go." I fake a smile for him, as I back toward the door.

"It's okay, we don't have to. That's not why I brought you here."

"It's not okay." I shake my head and fight back the tears threatening to spill.

"Don't leave like this. Let me at least calm you down. I can call you a cab," he offers, stepping closer and reaching out to me.

"I'm sorry." They are the only words I can manage as my hand fumbles with the handle of the door, and I rush out. Instead of waiting for the elevator, I take the stairs, running down all three flights to get to the foyer. When I step outside into the rain, I don't care that it soaks my hair. I don't care that each drop that lands on my skin reminds me of Garrett because these days, those kinds of memories, no matter how much they hurt, seem to be my only comfort.

I feel my purse vibrating and figure it must be Kieron calling. He didn't deserve that, the least I can do is offer him an explanation. I'll make one up for him tomorrow. Right now, I need to get home and cry into my pillow.

I manage to hail a cab, and after I get inside and give the driver my address, I breathe myself calm and realize how pathetic I am. I should take my roommate Savannah's advice and get myself a therapist. Everyone in L.A seems to have one. It's not right that after so much time I can't move on.

But I don't need a therapist to tell me why. I already know.

I *can't* move on because I don't *want* to.

I don't want to give up on the idea of me and Garrett being together. I was there, I felt what we had between us, and maybe I'm young, maybe I'm naive and stupid, but I already know I'll never have that with anyone else.

My cell keeps on buzzing, and I decide I should at least

message Kieron to apologize. I take it out from my purse, and when I see Wade's name flashing on the screen, I feel my heart leap into my throat. Me and Wade have stayed in touch over the years, but the fact he's called me so many times, suggests something's wrong. My trembling finger accepts the call, and as soon as I hear his voice, I know it's bad.

"Hey darlin'," he doesn't sound like his usual upbeat self. He sounds like he's about to deal me a hard blow.

"Garrett?" His name wobbles out from my lips, and I hold my breath while I wait for Wade to tell me what's happened.

"No, darlin', Garrett's fine. It's your mom I'm calling about."

"Mom? What's happened to her?" I've barely heard from my mom since I left Montana, three summers ago. She hasn't made the effort to come out here and visit me. I'm sure she's been far too busy ensuring her assets are secure.

"I'm sorry Maisie, but she's dead." It takes a few seconds for me to absorb the words he's just said, and when they do sink in, they hit like tidal wave.

"*Dead?*" I repeat the word, hoping I've heard him wrong.

"Yeah. I feel real shitty tellin' ya over the phone, but, I didn't want ya hearin' it from the sheriff."

"She can't be dead." I shake my head and close my eyes, trying to remember the last time we spoke. It's been so long, I can't even recall it.

She was always so self-absorbed that when we did catch up on the phone, she never took the time to ask about *my* life or how *I* was doing.

Truth is, I've always resented her. As a child I could never settle, I was constantly changing schools and having to make new friends to fit around her love life. I've resented her even more these past few years. I figure if she'd never dragged me away to the Carson Ranch, I would never have had my heart broken.

"Maisie, whatcha wanna do?" Hearing Wade's voice again, reminds me he's still on the line.

"The funeral." It suddenly dawns on me that I'll have to go back and face everything I left behind.

"Coroner says her body can be released once the police have all the evidence they need for their investigation. We're hoping it'll be sometime next week."

"Police?" I question, realizing that I haven't even asked what happened to her. Maybe I've become just as self-absorbed as she was.

"Sweetheart, your mom's death wasn't an accident. She was shot."

My breath catches in my throat, and my body goes cold.

"Maisie, ya still there?" Wade sounds concerned.

"I'm here." I force the words past my dry throat.

"Whatcha wanna do?" he asks me again, and as I stare out at the raindrops running down the window and blurring the city light, I realize there's only one thing I can do.

"I guess it's time for me to come back," I answer, weakly.

CHAPTER 2

GARRETT

"Jesus, ya antsy today." Wade sits back in the chair opposite mine and rests his boots on my desk. They're his special occasion boots, so they're clean, but I cold-stare him, anyway.

"C'mon, we're burying the witch. I'da thought you'd at least manage a smile."

"We'll have none of that talk when she gets here." I point my finger at him in warning before Dalton's knuckles tap the open door and interrupts us.

"I'm just about to head to the airport to pick up Maisie. I spoke to Grahame, and you were right. She's got a room booked at the guest house." He confirms my suspicions.

"She's cutting it fine. You'll have to take her straight to the funeral." Wade cranes his neck, to look back at him.

"And after?" Dalton's looking at me now.

"You take her wherever she wants to go." I look down at my desk to avoid the look I know they're both gonna be givin' me.

"Sure thing, boss." Dalton leaves, but I still feel Wade's eyes judging me.

"*What?*" I eventually glance up at him.

"Nothin'." He shakes his head, curling his lip like he's amused by my suffering.

"Whatcha expect me to do? Throw the girl over my

shoulder at her mom's funeral and force her to come back here?"

The look on Wade's face suggests that's exactly what he expects.

"Sounds like the kinda thing Garrett Carson *would* do. We both know you're not gonna let her leave here a second time. Fucking hell, Gar... it's been three years, and I ain't even seen you look at another woman. You know what you want, and now's your chance to get it."

Wade readjusts his hat to cover his eyes, so all I got left to see is the clever smirk that I want to punch off his face.

"You're right, I ain't gonna let her leave town again. But I'm not going in caveman style. I'm trying a new approach. I'm giving her space."

"Space?" Wade bursts out laughing. "I think the two of you have had more than enough space." Getting up from the chair, he heads for the door.

"Where ya going?"

"I'm picking up Leia and her sister, and taking them to the funeral. Her mom and dad have been away, so they're heading straight there." He starts fixing up his tie in the mirror.

"And why ain't Leia ridin' with her fiancé?" I'm in a shit mood, so I don't even feel guilty for knocking the pride off his face.

"Caleb's at a conference, so he can't make it."

"So, you're steppin' in?" Now it's my turn to look smug as I stand up and round my desk, stepping behind my brother and looking over his shoulder into our reflection.

"I'm not gonna take relationship advice from a man who's lived in the same town as the girl he's in love with his whole life, and *still* hasn't made his move." I brush some imaginary lint off his suit jacket and smile before I head out the door.

"Fuck you!" he yells after me, and I shake my head and laugh before heading out to the bunkhouse.

"Boss." Otis sits up on his bunk and tips his chin when I let myself in, while Finn and Tate share a glance with each other that I don't like the look of.

"Where's Mitch?" I scan the room, looking for my head wrangler.

"We told him not to go." Finn speaks up first, earning himself a sharp jab from Tate's elbow.

"Go where?"

"He's at the Mason Ranch. One of their wranglers was talkin' shit about you at the auction this morning, it got back to him, and well..." I don't need Finn to explain any further.

"Fuck," I sigh as I head straight back out the door, slamming it behind me and marching toward my truck. This is the last thing I need today. I'm already nervous as hell about seeing Maisie again. My plan to give her space was easier to come up with than it will be to execute.

I get in my truck and start the engine, pulling off and heading for the Mason Ranch. When I get there, I follow the sound of chaos that's coming from one of the stables.

"I'll teach you what happens to folk who slander my boss." Mitch lays a heavy blow of his fist into the guy on the floor. There's a few of Mason's wranglers here to witness, but none who look like they're gonna do anything about it. You can tell they're green, not just by how young they look, but by the condition of the Stetsons on their heads and the boots on their feet. The leather ain't worn, and they barely got a scuff between 'em.

"Hey Mitch, c'mon. Not today." I reach down, pulling at his shoulder and holding him back.

"Every day, Garrett. Every-fuckin'-day!" He snarls at the

beaten-up cowboy, who's laid out on the ground, before he spits on him.

"Only sayin' what everyone else is thinkin'." The piece of shit on the floor shows he's got some balls, and when Mitch leaps to go at him again, I manage to hold him back.

"We gotta funeral to get to," I remind him. He knows today's important. The whole town will be watching to see how the Carsons react to Cora's death. We ain't got time for petty scraps.

I hold out my hand to help the guy up from the floor, and he takes it with a cocky look toward Mitch. Then I wait until he's on his feet before grabbing the front of his shirt and shoving him into one of the empty stalls. I slam him hard against the wall and get right in his face.

"Don't concern yourself with who killed that gold-diggin' whore. Concern yourself with the fact that if my name leaves your mouth again, you'll be as dead as she is." I could punch his lights out, but he's already beaten black and blue, and since I don't wanna get blood on the only decent suit I own, I let him go. Turning my back on him, I pick up Mitch's hat from where it's fallen and hand it back to him.

"Back to work boys, that horseshit ain't gonna shovel up itself," I tell the spectators as I head back to my truck with Mitch, and we both stare across the yard toward the main house. The Mason family are gathered on their porch with their fancy town car parked outside, waiting to take them to the funeral. Ronnie Mason puts on his sunglasses and is followed by his eldest son Joe and his wife, Aubrey, as he steps toward it. She's the only one of them who notices we're here, and she offers me a tiny smile before she lowers her head to look at the ground again.

Fair play to Cole, he's stuck it out here, and he's done it all for her. We didn't think he'd last the first winter, but he proved us wrong. Just shows how determined and stubborn us Carson men can be.

Still, I can't help wondering if what he's doing here brings them both more pain than comfort. Aubrey ain't ever gonna leave her husband, the way she looks at him like she fears him suggests she couldn't, even if she wanted to.

"You good?" Mitch asks, shaking me out of my thoughts.

"Yeah, I'm good," I assure him, getting behind the wheel and starting the engine. I give him a look once he gets in beside me, one that suggests I got more to say.

"Don't start. I'm too old in the tooth for lectures, and I ain't ever gonna change my ways." He lights himself up a smoke and hangs his arm out the window, as I drive on.

"Don't mind us. Just offerin' ya staff some neighborly advice," he calls out the window, raising his hat as we drive past the Mason family toward the gate.

"I'm surprised Finn and Tate didn't go with ya," I snigger. Mitch is right. You can't teach an old dog new tricks, there are some that will never be tame, and he's the best of 'em.

"They wanted to, but I ordered 'em to stay behind. Last thing ya needed today was a bunkhouse brawl. I delivered the warnin' that was needed."

I nod back and focus on the road, trying not to think about what's coming. We ain't got time to go back to the ranch, we're gonna have to head straight to the funeral, and I still don't feel ready to face Maisie yet.

"It's gonna be okay, ya know. The girl's gonna know ya didn't do it."

"I don't care if she thinks I did it, or not." I know my lie won't stick with the man I've known my whole life, but I tell it anyway.

"Boy, your horse shit stinks worse than the Mason's yard. I think that girls' opinion is about the only one you *do* care about.

This is your chance to right your wrongs. All good men make mistakes, but smart ones don't make 'em twice." He blows out a huge cloud of smoke and laughs.

I pull up at the cemetery and look at the chairs that are set up around, what will be, Cora's final resting place. Nobody's here yet, just the priest who's waiting to greet us. I pull down my visor and look at the picture of Maisie, I keep there. I don't care if Mitch sees it. He knows how I feel about the girl. Everybody fucking knows.

She's beautiful, far too good for a man who's got what I have on his conscience, but Mitch and Wade are both right. This is my chance, the only one I'm likely to get. Nothing holds Maisie to this town anymore, and if I let her leave again, she's never coming back.

I snap the visor back up and look across at Mitch.

"Whatever it takes," I tell him, watching a smile rise on his lips.

"I was hoping you'd say that." He flicks his smoke out the window and chuckles to himself before getting out.

CHAPTER 3

MAISIE

I spend the entire service trying not to look at him, but it's impossible. Garrett Carson hasn't changed a bit. He's just as tall, just as handsome, and just like I feared, the draw I have to go to him is still there. Leia stands beside me and holds my hand. She's another person from Fork River I've stayed in touch with, and she's even visited me a few times in L.A.

I feel her squeeze my hand tight, as the priest says his words, and when the mayor stands up to say a few words of his own. Mom would be devastated to miss all this fuss.

Maybe I should be thinking about other things, like the fact she's gone, and that I'll never see her again. Maybe I should be wondering who it was that put an end to her life. But all I can focus on is him. When I brave glancing up from the ground, to where he's standing on the other side of her casket, his hands are crossed respectfully in front of him, and although his head is low, his eyes are on me.

Those heavy, alluring eyes that have haunted my dreams since I left, and the power inside them, almost makes me gasp. Leia hands me a tissue, and it reminds me that I should be crying. My mother is dead. The woman who gave birth to me, and raised me, is about to be put in the ground. But I feel no sadness and suffer no loss because the truth is, I lost my mom a long time ago. Way before we came here.

Thinking about it, I never really had her.

My mom has never, in her tragically-too-short life, put me first and looking around at all these people who knew her for such a short time and are grieving her loss, makes me wonder why I'm actually here.

When the service is over, and people start heading back to their cars, I feel an arm wrap around my shoulder.

"It's good to see ya girl. Sorry it's like this." Wade kisses my cheek and smiles at me sadly when I look at him.

"Did Dalton manage to contain his excitement 'bout seeing ya?" he asks, and I smile a little when I recall the greeting he gave me back at the airport. He'd lifted me off my feet and spun me around like we were reunited lovers.

"Not so well." I let Wade lead me away from the graveyard toward the truck where Dalton is leaning on the hood, waiting for me.

"Mom and Dad are having a thing back at their place," Leia informs me, trying to sound enthusiastic. "Garrett offered to do something back at the ranch, but given the circumstances, it didn't seem appropri…" I notice the way Wade shakes his head to cut her off.

"What do you mean not appropriate?"

"Hell, Leia, ya ever think before you speak?" Wade rolls his eyes as he nervously loosens his tie.

"Look darlin', Garrett and your mom did a lotta head butting, in fact, she made our lives kinda hell. The police cleared him, but people round town are talkin', and they're pretty convinced it was him who…"

"Wait. People think Garrett killed my mom?" I feel my knees buckle, but somehow, I manage to stay on my feet.

"That's what they're sayin', but I'm tellin' ya, it ain't true," Wade assures me, and when I hear the low, gravelly sound of a throat clearing behind me, I instantly know who it belongs to.

15

"Garrett." His name leaks desperately from my mouth as I turn around to face him, and I blush when I realize what a fuck-up I've just made of our first encounter. I was supposed to show courage and strength, not weakness.

"Maisie." He raises his hat slightly from his head and looks me over, the same way he always used to. When his eyes glance over my shoulder at Leia and Wade, they both excuse themselves and leave the two of us in an awkward stare-off.

"How long ya in town for?" Garrett eventually breaks the silence, and I notice the slight edge of nervousness in his tone.

"I leave tomorrow afternoon, I got an appointment in Billings tomorrow morning with Mom's lawyer, and then I'm flying straight back." I have to twiddle my fingers to try and stop them from reaching out to him.

He nods slowly, taking in what I said but not reacting to it.

"It was kind of you to send Dalton to fetch me. Thank you." I smile awkwardly.

"How did you know I sent him?" He questions, narrowing his eyes and making it so hard for me to hate him the way I should.

"He told me you did," I admit, and it breaks the ice because we both smirk a little when I glance across at him. Dalton never was good at hiding anything. He's wearing black like all the other mourners today, but that huge smile of his hasn't dropped from his face since he's been here.

"I hear you're staying at the Taylor's." Garrett quickly turns the conversation serious again. I can see the tension in his hands as he clenches his fists, and I try not to be distracted by remembering how they felt, touching me.

"Yeah, I don't think I'm gonna go to the Walker's place. If it's okay with you, I'll ask Dalton to give me a ride back to the guest house now." I pull a smile together for him, and when he nods back at me, I turn and walk away.

"Come home." I hear the words he blurts out from behind me, but I have to turn around to believe he said them, and when I do, he's the one who looks embarrassed as he clears his throat again.

"I mean, don't stay at the guest house. You got a room at the ranch." I watch him swallow his pride while he waits for my answer.

"Garrett, I don't think..." He silences me when he steps forward and presses his finger over my lips. A combination of his cologne, mixed with cigarettes and leather, invade my nostrils, reminding me of all the little things I've missed about him.

"The ranch is your home, you belong there, not at the guesthouse. I'll sleep in the bunkhouse tonight if it'll make ya more comfortable." I look up at him, trying to form words but failing, and when I shake my head, the look of disappointment that spreads over his handsome features makes me desperate to kiss him again.

"Maisie, please don't be stubborn. I want you to come home tonight, but I won't beg," he warns, and as much as he deserves to suffer for what he did to me, I take the high road and put him out of his misery.

Clutching at his wrist I pull his hand away from my mouth and feel his finger drag my lip, as it slips away.

"What I meant is, that there's no need for you to sleep in the bunkhouse. We're both adults, right?" I manage to pull some sass together as I turn my back on him for a second time and walk towards Dalton.

"Where to my lady?" he asks, as he opens up the passenger door for me.

"To the Carson Ranch." I hop up into the seat and buckle myself in, ignoring the huge, victorious smile on Dalton's face, and trying not to stare in the wing mirror when he shuts the door.

Of course I fail, and when I see Garrett in the reflection standing and staring, with that look on his face that tells me I pissed him off, I feel a little victorious myself.

S he's only been back in town five minutes, and she's sending me crazy already. The kinda crazy I've missed.

I make sure I get back to the house before she does, and I head straight for my room to get out of my suit and into something more practical.

I manage to make it out into the stables before Dalton pulls up, and when Tate steps into the stables and catches me watching her stepping on to the porch, I try and make myself look busy.

"Wasn't expecting her to come back here," he mentions casually, as he takes a saddle and throws it over Hooter's back.

"Wade say ya could ride his horse?" I check, trying to change the subject.

"He called and asked me to get him saddled. Sounded kinda tense," Tate explains as he continues to get Hooter ready.

"Miss Wildman's home, boss." Dalton steps into the stable, looking pleased with himself.

"Make sure she's got everything she needs. She probably wants to rest and have some time to herself." I grab my own saddle and head over toward Thunder. Wade's got the right idea about riding out, and I wanna get a head start on him. The last thing I need is company, and I sure as shit don't wanna lecture from him on how I'm already fuckin' this up.

Maisie leaves tomorrow, I ain't got the time to be wasting, but being around her feels too intense. I gotta get my head on straight before I can attempt any kinda conversation I need to have with her.

"I don't know about that, boss. I think she'd like your company very much," Dalton points out, and Tate rubs his finger under his nose to try and hide the snigger on his lips.

"Just make sure she's comfortable." I sling my leg over Thunder's back and pull myself up, clicking him on and trotting out the yard.

I stay out as late as I can, trying to think of the words I should say. I haven't spoken a single word to her since she left. I never ask Wade about her in case I don't like what I hear. I can only assume she has someone back in L.A. It would be impossible for a pretty girl like her not to. I've laid awake at night, staring at my ceiling and torturing myself with thoughts of who she might be with. I think about the faceless man touching her skin and kissing her lips, and the only way to make the pain stop is to think about killing him for it.

My soul isn't quite black enough for me to kid myself that I have the right to those kinda thoughts.

I have no rights to her.

I know I'm being unreasonable. But there's nothing reasonable about the man I've become, and Maisie Wildman is about to get a taste of that man. Because I've already figured that there are no limits I won't go to to keep her here.

I take Thunder back to the stable and leave him for Otis to settle before I take a deep breath and head inside the house. I don't expect to find her quite so soon. She's laying on the couch sleeping, and I'm grateful for the chance I get to admire her without her judgment.

I rest my ass on the oak coffee table in front of her and study her face. The years haven't changed her, her skin is still smooth and slightly sunkissed. Her nose is still fuckin' adorable and looking at her lips still makes me hungry for 'em. She's been crying, I can tell from the smudge of makeup under her eyelashes, and as desperate as I am to wipe those smudges away, I'm petrified of waking her. I can't remember the last time I was scared about anything. Yet a few hours of having this dainty, little thing back in my life's got me terrified.

Her lashes start to flutter, and when her eyes slowly open, I'm the first thing she sees.

I like that it makes her smile.

"Hey." Her soft whisper travels down my spine and makes it tingle. I wanna reach out and grab her, to hold her tight and never fuckin' let go. But I know that ain't the way with her. Maisie likes me to take control, but she needs to know she's in charge of the brakes.

"Hey." I shift back a little when I realize how close I've got to her face.

"I must have dropped off. How late is it?" She sits up and wearily looks around the room.

"It's supper time. I gave Josie the day off, so you'll have to stand for my cooking, I'm afraid," I warn her with a smile that I hope will make her feel at ease around me again.

"I'm sure I'll manage." She turns her body so it's facing mine and runs her hands through her long blonde waves.

"You've been cryin'," I state the fuckin' obvious and feel like a fool for it when she laughs.

"My mom just died." Her big, blue eyes sparkle from her unshed tears as she stares back at me, and it does nothing to stop me from feeling like a dick.

"I never told ya that I was sorry about that." I close my eyes and link my hands together.

"Are you, really?" She don't sound convinced, and when I open my eyes, she don't look it either. "Wade already told me she made your life hell." She teases her hair over to one side and looks as if she's waiting on a response.

"Are you asking me if I killed her?" I hold her stare, and for the first time in a long while, I start to feel alive again. That spark that was always there between us rushes through my veins and targets straight for my chest.

"You had a motive," she points out, taking a risk and edging closer to me.

"And d'ya really think I'd be capable of hurtin' a woman?" I question, shifting closer myself. We're just inches apart from each other now, and kissing her would be so easy.

"You hurt me." Her words douse me with cold water, and it makes me pull away again. When she stands up and starts heading for the stairs I wanna chase after her. I wanna pin her down and make her listen to me, but knowing I ain't got the words, I have to let her go.

I watch her take the stairs, and walk across the landing before she disappears into her room and slams the door.

It's a few hours later when I knock on her bedroom door to tell her supper's ready. When she comes out she's changed, from the black dress she was wearing, into a pair of jeans and a tee that's far too tight and far too short not to be distracted by.

"Dinner's ready," I growl at her, and when she smiles at me like nothing good or bad ever happened between us, it makes the frustration inside me reach boiling point.

Why do I wanna keep her so bad when all she does is infuriate me?

She steps past me and heads down the stairs, and I follow after her.

"Not in there." I stop her before she steps into the dining room, and I open the kitchen door instead. "Seemed silly layin' that huge table just for the two of us," I tell her a partial truth. What I leave out is the fact I don't want any space between us tonight. Wade's right, we've had far too much of it. I hold the door for her while she steps inside, and she can't hide the look of surprise on her face when she sees what's in front of her.

I found a round tablecloth in a basket, in the pantry, and lit some of the candles we use when the power cuts out. Sure, the flowers on the table ain't roses, but they're all we had growing in the yard, and they're pretty. I even finished the last of the whiskey so I could use the bottle for a vase.

"I was gonna cook, but I only know one recipe and didn't think you'd go for cowboy casserole." I step past her and pull out a chair.

"So, what have we got?" She takes the seat I offer and tries real hard to hide the smile from her face.

"I sent one of the boys into town, Dolores makes the best brisket cobbler you'll ever taste." I use a mitt to take the foil tray out of the oven where I've been heating it and rest it on the table. Maisie don't look all that impressed but she does seem amused, which I guess stands for something.

"What is all this, Garrett?" she asks as I cut into the cobbler and serve some onto her plate. I serve myself some and pour the wine before I even attempt to answer her.

"This is me askin' ya to give me some more time." I decide it's stupid to run before I walk. I hurt Maisie when I sent her away, and I need to build up her trust before I expect anything else of her.

"We've had a lot of time, Garrett, three years of it." She picks up her fork and digs in, looking at me for more of those damn fucking words and enjoying every second of my suffering.

"I shouldn't have let ya leave," I admit, getting straight to the point. It ain't easy for a Carson man to admit where he went wrong but pride ain't gonna stop me from making right on my wrongs.

"*Let* me leave?" She raises her eyebrows, and now she's just being bratty.

"You know what I mean, Maisie, and I understand that I'm three years too late with all this shit, but I've had three years of hurt and wonderin', and I don't want three more. I'm askin' ya to cancel your flight and give me a week to convince you that I can give you a better life here, than whatever you got back home." I lay it all out on the overdressed fuckin' table for her and watch as her mouth drops open and her eyes get bigger.

She quickly pulls herself back together again, though.

"What's changed? Am I old enough for you now?" She tilts her head and picks up the wine that she can now legally drink.

"There was way more to it than that, Maisie, and you fuckin' know it."

"So, I'll ask again. What's changed?"

I wanna swipe my arm across this table and fuck her sassy, little ass over it. She can see I'm trying, and she's purposely making it hard for me.

"Me. I've changed," I confess, "I knew what I wanted back then, but I was scared of it."

"And you're not scared anymore?" She laughs at me.

"Yeah, I'm scared." If it's my fear she wants, it's all hers, I spent too long denying my feelings to myself. I won't hold back on the truth now.

"But I ain't about to let it stop it from getting what I want," I warn her.

"And what is it, exactly, that you *do* want?" She twists her fork into her food like it's my fuckin' heart that she's playing with, and I reach across the table, take her hand, forcing her to drop it.

"I want you, here with me. I want you to be mine. I wanna make ya smile the way Dalton and Wade do, and I want us to fill this house with beautiful, sassy, stubborn kids."

"Kids?" She chokes on her food and stares back at me in shock.

"Yeah, Maisie, kids, loads of 'em. I'll tell you what's changed. Letting you go made me sit back and re-evaluate everything. I asked myself a lotta questions about what I wanted, and all of 'em had you in the answer. I realized that I want to be happy, and I need ya here for that to happen. That's what's changed. Gimme a week, and I'll make you realize that you belong here with me." Maisie doesn't even blink as she listens to my speech, and when I'm done, I slowly release her hand and watch her try to absorb everything I just said.

That smart-assed smile isn't on her face anymore. If anything, she looks a little scared herself, and when she slowly stands up from the table, I'm sure I've fuckin' blown it.

I came on too strong. I wasn't supposed to mention the kids part so soon. But once I opened up the stalls, I got all passionate and shit.

Maisie surprises me when she rounds the table to stand beside me, and when I turn my body towards hers and stand up, towering over her and looking down for her response, she smiles.

"Well, Garrett Carson, let's see what you got." She doesnt give me a chance to kiss her the way I want to, she backs away and leaves me like a starved wolf as she walks out the door.

I head down to breakfast with a spring in my step and a smile on my face. I thought coming back here would be hard. Turns out Garrett has suffered just as much as me, and now he wants to make it right. I want to let him, but that doesn't mean I should make it easy on him.

"Mornin'." Wade greets me with a grin, as I grab a bowl of muesli and join him at the table.

"Where did you get to last night? You missed one hell of a dinner." I ask sarcastically, looking to the head of the table where Garrett is already sitting. He folds up his paper and rests it beside his plate before subtly shaking his head at his brother.

"Had other plans," Wade tells me, with a wide smile that absolutely confirms he's lying.

"What time's your appointment?" Garrett pours me some juice.

"It's at ten," I answer, already liking the way he's taking care of me.

"Great, I'll drive ya. We can grab some lunch in Billings after."

"I already have a ride, Leia's taking me, and we're gonna do some shopping, but thanks for the offer." I shrug my shoulders and raise my glass as a thank you, before taking a sip. I can tell from the look on Wade's face that he wants to high-five me across the table, but we both refrain.

My cell starts to vibrate on the table, and I silence it when I see Kieron's name flashing. He hasn't stopped calling me since that night at his new apartment, and to avoid the awkward conversation I know I'll have to have with him, I've been using my mother's death as an excuse.

I notice the snarl Garrett makes, when the name flashes up for a second time.

"You should answer that, whoever it is seems eager to get hold of ya." When he swallows, all the muscles in his neck tense, and he clutches his cutlery tight in his fist.

"It's nothing that can't wait," I bite back cheerily, before taking another sip of juice. I'd forgotten how much sweeter it tastes here.

"As much as I'd like to stay among this weird, sexual tension thing you've got happenin' here, there's work to do." Wade picks up his hat and places it on his head before he leaves us.

There's a long silence while we both eat, and when my cell rings for a third time, I can feel the frustration coming off Garrett in flames. But I'm still shocked as hell when he picks it up and answers it.

"What?" he growls down the phone, scrunching his napkin in his fist and slamming it on the table.

"Maisie's not available right now." His eyes stare into mine, daring me to say otherwise.

"Who am I?" A slight grin pulls on his face. "I'm her boyfriend." He raises an eyebrow at me, as if he dares me to argue with that too, and it takes all my willpower not to smirk at how fucking good that sounds.

"If ya call her again, I'll find out where ya are, and I'll make ya choke on my fist." He hangs up and tosses my cell back on the table, before picking up his fork and continuing to eat.

I stare at him in shock, and when I start to laugh, he looks up at me blankly. "Ya find something amusing?"

I smile when I realize he's back to being the Garrett I fell in love with. Any grovel he had in him is up and gone, and I kinda like it. It didn't suit him anyway.

"Don't you think that was a little too much?" I bite my lip to try and tame my amusement, and when Garrett gets up and places his hat on, the same way Wade did, he steps behind me and leans down to whisper in my ear.

"We're just gettin' started, baby." He kisses my cheek before leaving, and as much as I want to chase after him and beg him to show me what he means, I have to hold back.

I want to trust him, but it's hard to forget how much he hurt me, and if Garrett is one thing, it's unpredictable. I can't jump in feet first, this time. I can't let him break my heart into any more pieces and so, I stay in my seat. I finish my breakfast, and I wait for Leia to get here, so I can fill her in on everything that's happened since I left her at the funeral.

"So that's it, he just announced he was your boyfriend and hung up?" Leia looks perplexed, as I explain.

"Yep, just like that," I shrug, as I read through all the paperwork Mom's lawyer had sent to me in L.A. I haven't told Garrett or Wade that Mom left the shares she had in the ranch to me. I'm just gonna have her lawyer put everything back in their name and forget about it. I don't want anything that came from her, I've still got the $50,000 inheritance I got from Bill in a savings account, and I will find a way of getting that back to the Carson brothers, who should have had it in the first place.

"I guess you could say it's romantic." She pulls a face that suggests she doesn't think that at all, and I quit trying to figure out all the words on the document and decide to change the subject.

"So, when's the big day?" I look at the huge rock on her finger. I briefly met Caleb Mason at Mom and Bill's wedding, and I can remember him being handsome, which is good, considering he has no personality whatsoever.

"April. Mom's insisting we have a spring wedding," she tells me excitedly.

"And what does Wade say about it all?" I slam my hand over my mouth the moment the question leaves my lips.

"Wade?" Leia laughs. "He's happy for me. What else would he have to say?" Her response proves she's still clueless about how he feels, and it reminds me to have a conversation with him to check how he's dealing with this.

"Nothing, I just know the two of you are close, that's all." I recover quickly, and when Leia pulls up outside the lawyer's office, I get out the car before I can put my foot in my mouth again. "I'll be half an hour, tops. I'll call when I'm done."

"Don't forget we need to find you an outfit to wear to my engagement party," she reminds me, wiggling her fingers to show off the ring again, before she pulls off.

I spend twenty minutes in Harold Sengar's reception before his secretary calls me through, and when he stands up and reaches across his desk to shake my hand, I can see why Mom refused to use anyone else but him. He's handsome for an old guy, and he's got that sophisticated charm that Mother has always been attracted to.

"Maisie, it's nice to finally meet you, please take a seat." He gestures for me to sit as he sits back down, and before he can start or convince me that I'm stupid, I explain what I need him to do.

"I need my shares to be returned to the Carson brothers, split three ways between them all. I know the name of the lawyer they use, and I'm relying on your and Miles' discretion when it comes to telling them where it came from."

"Miss Wildman, do you understand the value of those shares?" Harold frowns at me, like I need to get my head checked.

"Yes, I understand fully, but I don't want them. I'm nothing like my mother. I don't like how she operated, and I certainly don't wish to benefit from it. I want all my shares in the Copper Ridge Ranch transferred," I tell him again, standing firm.

"*All* your shares?" he checks, with an even bigger look of shock on his face. "Even the ones that were transferred to you last year?"

"Last year? You must be mistaken. I inherited a ten percent share that was my mother's. I want that transferred back to the Carsons."

"And you wish to keep the other fifteen percent?" He looks confused.

"I don't have any more shares in Copper Ridge," I explain, for a second time, wondering where he's getting mixed up.

"Maisie, the information I have here, tells me differently. You had a fifteen percent stake, and upon your mother's death you now have a further ten. I may not be your lawyer, ma'am, but it would be unethical of me not to tell you what you're giving up here."

"Where the hell are you getting this fifteen percent from?" I scrub my hands over my face, trying to add all this up.

"It was transferred into your name last year. You would have signed a transfer form."

"Well, I didn't. I didn't sign anything," I assure him, and he checks over the paperwork in front of him again before he looks up at me and sighs.

"I don't know what's happened, ma'am, but there has been no mistake here. You own twenty-five percent of the Copper Ridge Ranch, and that makes you an equal stakeholder. My suggestion is, you leave here and think about what you do. Don't make any rash decisions here. Your shares are worth a fortune."

I leave Harold's office with my head spinning. None of this makes any sense. I can only assume these other shares came from Garrett, but why would he risk the thing that's most important to him? I can't imagine his brothers being all too happy about it, either.

I meet up with Leia and decide not to mention anything to her.

I need to get my head around this myself first, and I need to speak to Garrett.

I struggle to focus as we search for a dress for me to wear to Leia's engagement party, and I'm not entirely convinced that the sequin dress we leave the boutique with, is my style but I'm too shocked to argue with her. When she drops me back off at the ranch and drives away, I look across the yard to where Garrett is riding around the corral, spinning his rope and catching up calves so they can be branded by Tate and Mitch.

It's scary how the time that's passed between us seems irrelevant now, and it's even crazier how fast a broken heart can start to heal.

Garrett pulls Thunder to a stop when he catches me watching him, and as he smiles, raising his hand to the rim of his hat and tipping his head, that warm fuzzy feeling I never thought I'd get back fills my stomach. I can feel it happening all too quickly, the ground whipping from under my feet again, and all I can do is smile back at the man who has the potential to ruin me and pray to God I don't fall too hard.

CHAPTER 6

GARRETT

It's been a long day, and it will be another long one tomorrow. I feel bad for leaving the boys to finish up, but there have to be some perks to being the boss, and I'd like to eat with Maisie again tonight.

She's sitting up on the worktop talking to Josie when I get in, and the way she lowers her head when she sees me makes me wonder if I've done something wrong.

"Hard day Mr. Carson?" Josie asks, kneading the bread she's making and blowing the hair out of her face.

"You could say that. I'm gonna take a shower and have an hour takin' care of paperwork shit."

"Perfect, I'll set the table for eight." She smiles and gets back to work, while Maisie refuses to acknowledge me.

It bothers me. I can't imagine what I've done to piss her off since I haven't seen her properly since breakfast.

Maybe she considered me answering her phone too invasive. I've never been in a relationship before. How am I supposed to know the rules?

I take a shower and head down to my office to place some orders and pay the vet and farrier bills. This is the side of ranching that I hate. The kinda shit my grandfather never had to deal with, and I've only been at it for a few minutes when the door opens, and Maisie charges through it like she wants to get something off her chest.

"Why?" She crosses her arms over her chest and scowls at me.

"Hey darlin'. How was your day?" I smile at her sarcastically and wait for her to bite.

"Don't play dumb. Why have you given me fifteen percent of your shares? Garrett, you can't just *give* someone something like that."

"Yes, you can." I shrug, trying to avoid the answer to her question. It's not something I wanna get into, and if I tell her the truth, it sure ain't gonna help my cause keeping her here.

"Garrett. If you want to prove to me that I can trust you, there can be no secrets." She warns, looking serious as hell.

"Can't ya just say thank you and be done with it?" I sigh, leaning back in my chair and running my finger across my bottom lip. Maisie looks hot as sin today, her hair is styled in a cute braid that hangs over her shoulder, and that frustrated look on her face is putting unholy thoughts in my head.

"Garrett." She lets out a long sigh and rounds my desk, hopping up and resting her ass on the surface in front of me. The look on her face tells me she ain't in the mood to play games.

"I wanted you to have those shares in case anything happens to me," I confess, staring down at the rips in her jeans to avoid having to look at her. She places her hand under my chin and forces me to look up.

"Why? I'm nothing to you. Those shares belong to your brothers."

"You don't get it, do ya?" I shake my head and laugh at her, "You're everything to me. I told ya, I know what I want, and once that happens, there's nothing that will stop me from gettin' it. I want you taken care of. Whether I'm here to do that myself or not."

"Do you know how morbid this sounds?" She stares back at me angrily. "What makes you think anything's gonna happen to you?"

"Things have changed since you left. There's a certain way this ranch is run now. I let ya leave because I didn't want to bring you into it. But I've figured that not havin' you ain't an option. You're part of this too. Those shares were mine to give away, my brothers knew about it, and I had their blessing."

"And how, exactly, are things running now?" She's got a curious look on her face.

"The Carsons don't take no shit. We have our own laws and our own justice system." I explain it the best way I can. Last thing I wanna do is scare her.

"My mom left me the ten percent she inherited from your father. I'm an equal shareholder now." The way she bites her lip suggests she's worried about how I'm gonna react to that fact.

"Good, then you should be pulling your weight around here. I hate this office and this laptop. Ya think you could figure it out?" I look up at her cleverly.

"I did some billings and accounts for the gallery." When she rolls her eyes, I know she aint gonna stay mad at me for long.

"Great, I'd appreciate the help." I'm hoping that'll be the end of it, but I should know better.

"How did you transfer them without me knowing?" She frowns. "And what if I'd never come back? Garrett, we don't know if this is gonna work out. It's a huge deal giving me something like this, and I don't know how to feel about accepting it." She confesses, looking overwhelmed, and I can't exactly blame her. I've laid a lot on her in the 24 hours she's been back in town.

"I don't have to tell ya that Miles ain't a normal kinda lawyer, I tell him what I need, and he gets the job done. I don't ask no questions. If you wanna know, you'll have to ask him that yourself. And I wouldn't have ever regretted those shares bein' yours, not even if you didn't come back. I got a reminder when you were here about what this place was all about. It's about building a future and leaving something behind for those you care about. I put all this in place over a year ago when I had no hope in you comin' back because it felt like the right thing to do, and nothing's gonna change my mind about that decision. Not even if you walked out of that door now and never came back again." I tell her, keeping a serious look on my face so she knows that I mean every single word.

"You know you're crazy? Normal guys find a girl they like, they take her on a few dates, see how things work out. Not you. You break a girl's heart, you leave her suffering for three years, then tell her you want her babies and give her half your assets."

"Yeah well, normal gets boring real quick," I tell her, pulling my chair a little closer to where she's sitting. I wanna kiss her. I wanna lay her back on my desk and take from her everything I've wanted for these long three years I've spent without her. But there's something I need to know, even if it's gonna hurt.

"Who's Kieron?" The smile drops off her face when I ask, convincing me that he means something to her.

It ain't my place to be jealous, not when I was the one who told her to move on. When I let her go, I knew there would be consequences to my actions.

But jealous is exactly what I'm feeling right now, and I'm feeling so much of it that I could tear down fucking walls.

"He's someone I was seeing back in L.A." she admits, sliding off my desk and backing away from me like she's scared.

"Did you like him?" I sink the blade a little deeper into my own flesh by asking more.

"I wouldn't have been seeing him if I didn't like him." She tries being smart, and I feel my pulse beat faster.

"Don't be clever." I shake my head and scrub my hand over my face. I don't know who this Kieron guy is but the thought of him, and all the men who could have come before him, touching her, makes me wanna go on a rampage.

"Was he your first?" There's a voice screaming in my head, telling me to stop asking questions that I'm not gonna like the answer to, and as I stand up and move towards her, the tears that are filling her eyes suggest she doesn't want to answer me.

"No." She looks down at the fucking floor like she's ashamed.

"How many were there?" I hate myself for asking, but the sick asshole side of me needs to know.

"I don't want to talk about it." Maisie's lips remain tight.

"No secrets. That's a rule *you* made, remember?" I remind her. The last thing I wanna think about is Maisie being touched by anyone other than me. But these past years it's all I've tortured myself with.

"None." When she looks up, tears are streaming down her cheeks, and there's a look of hatred in her eyes that feels like a throat punch. "There have been none," she repeats viciously, trying so hard to keep the look on her face brave, but failing. "And that isn't because I haven't tried. Believe me. I wanted to fuck you out of my head so bad. I wanted to fix all the hurt you caused me. But I couldn't because every time I tried, you were all I could think about. You, and how it should have been. I really hope that makes you feel better." She turns on her heels and storms out, and despite feeling like the world's biggest asshole, I march up the stairs and follow her into her room.

"What are you doing, Garrett?" She asks, shaking her head

and wiping her eyes, and this time I don't bother to explain myself. I move toward her, grabbing her face in my palm and kissing her the way I've been wanting to for three long years. Any resistance she had soon fades when my tongue forces into her mouth, and she gives into me. She lets me give back what I took away from us, and it feels too fucking good to be real.

"Garrett." She eventually pushes me away, trying to catch her breath, and for a few seconds a look passes between us. One that says it's time to stop playing games and that we've both suffered more than enough.

I kiss her again, this time much more gently, and I'm surprised at how naturally it comes to me. I've never been gentle with a woman before. In fact, I don't think I've ever been gentle with anything. These hands weren't made for softness, but I made this girl a promise the day she left this ranch about how I'd make it for her if I was the man to take it, and I'm gonna make damn sure all that waiting she's done was worth it.

I lift her off her feet and wrap her legs around my waist, pushing her body back against her door and allowing my lips to taste the skin on her neck. I never forgot the way she smelt, and for days after she left, I'd come into this room just so I could take in that scent she left behind. It went away far too quickly, but now that she's back, I'll make sure it never leaves again.

Her hands grip me so tight, like she's afraid I'll let her go, and when I slide my nose up her neck and inhale her skin, she lets out a long relieved sigh.

"I get that you're mad at me, and I get that me tellin' ya that I'm pleased you didn't give yourself to anyone else is gonna make you a whole lot angrier. But what I'm tellin' ya now is that when you're ready, Maisie Wildman, I'll be waitin'." I whisper the words into her ear, pressing my hips deeper into hers and letting her feel what she does to me. I loosen the grip I've got on her thighs and let her feet drop to the floor before dragging myself away from her.

I hate being the man who hurt her, and I hate to think of the time she spent trying to heal herself. But I *will* be the man who fixes it, and Maisie Wildman will not regret waiting for me.

I head downstairs after supper is finished. I couldn't stomach eating anything. Since I came back, all my emotions have exhausted me. I don't feel like I'm grieving for my mom the way I should be. I came here looking for answers. I want to know who killed her and what the police are doing about it. But I've been so wrapped up in Garrett and the huge change of heart he's had, that I've put all that on hold.

I move straight for the kitchen to raid the fridge for some water, and find Wade sitting at the kitchen table, staring at the beer bottle in his hands.

"Something on your mind?" I grab myself one from the fridge and move over to join him.

"Too much." He gives me a sarcastic laugh and an unconvincing smile, as I sit opposite him.

"You wanna talk about it?" I pop the cap on my beer and take a mouthful. It's not my drink of choice, but it's all that seems to be in the fridge, and after the day I've had, alcohol is required.

"Talkin' ain't gonna fix it." He focuses on picking off the label on his bottle to avoid looking at me.

"I'm figuring this has something to do with Leia marrying Caleb Mason?"

"Ain't no flies on you, is there?" He looks up at me and

smirks, but I see the hurt in his eyes. "She asked me to go to their party on Friday night," he tells me sadly.

"You don't got a rodeo to be at?" I check.

"Quit last year." Wade's answer shocks me so much, I almost choke.

"What! Why? You loved what you did."

"It took me away from her, and after Pops died, I figured Garrett would need the help. Let's face it, Cole ain't comin' home anytime soon," he shrugs, still picking at the label.

"That was sweet of you." I reach across the table to take his hand in mine and can't help feeling sorry for him. Wade was living the dream riding broncos. Knowing he isn't doing it anymore, explains why the sparkle in his eyes is missing.

"*Sweet* ain't gettin' me nowhere. Leia's marryin' that bastard, and I'm gonna end up just like Cole, a bitter, twisted fuck who can't move on." He flicks his bottle cap at the trash can, and misses.

"It doesn't have to be that way." I try giving him some hope.

"You see how happy she is, you see that smile she's constantly got on her face? Why would I want to ruin that?" He shakes his head at me.

"You could tell her how you feel. Let her decide for herself," I suggest.

"Caleb Mason is an asshole, but he's the asshole she wants. I just gotta live with that." He slouches back in his chair and knocks back more of his beer.

"Jesus, here was me thinking you Carson men had some fire in your bellies. Turns out you're all just as pathetic as each other." Wade can wallow in self-pity if he wants, but I sure as hell won't be a spectator in it.

"Nothing's gonna change if you just sit back and let it happen. If you really love her, the least you can do is tell her.

Can't you see that you're all making the same mistake as each other?"

"Not all of us. It looks to me like Garrett's workin' pretty hard to try to fix his." He turns the table on our conversation. "Ya gonna take ya own advice and stop bein' stubborn?"

"I'm still here, aren't I?" I bite sarcastically, and wait for him to strike back.

"Just don't hurt him." He's staring across the table seriously at me, now. "Garrett's tough, the toughest fucker I know. But when it comes to you..." Wade shakes his head, like he doesn't quite know how to finish his own sentence.

"It's been hard for him without ya here."

"Why didn't you tell me about the shares, he said you knew. A heads up would have been nice."

"He didn't want ya to know about it unless ya had to. Maisie, half the time I never know what the hell goes through his head, but when it comes to you...I get it."

"You shouldn't give up on your dream. This place can manage without you, Wade." I get back to my point. I hate seeing him so deflated, it doesn't suit him.

"Question is, can I manage without this place?" he scratches his head and laughs to himself, again. "Don't matter how far away ya get; it just keeps summoning ya back. You're proof of that."

"Tell her, before it's too late." I stand up and kiss him on his cheek, before I leave him to think about all the pain he'll feel if he doesn't.

I notice a light on in the office when I go to head back upstairs, and knowing it will be Garrett that's in there, I push the door open wider. I find him staring at the laptop screen, drinking from a crystal glass, and he looks up at me as I step inside.

"Thank you," I keep my distance from him because if I get

close, I'll have to kiss him, and if I kiss him, I won't be able to think straight.

"For what?" He narrows his eyes at me, curiously.

"For the shares and for caring about me," I shrug, keeping my feet rooted to the spot where I'm standing, to stop myself from going to him.

"Ya welcome." He nods his head.

"Well, since I figure you're not gonna let me give them back, the least I could do is help out around here. I won't be throwing any ropes, or chewing on straw anytime soon, but I can do my share of work in here. So you can spend more time out there."

Garrett stands up, slowly stepping towards me, and uses the crook of his finger to push up my chin. When I look up at him, his rough thumb tenderly strokes my cheek. "And what if I want to spend my time with you?" he asks in that low, raspy voice that makes my insides melt.

"Then you better make time to take me riding. I've missed it," I smile, and when he uses the finger he's got under my chin, to draw me up to his lips, and a soft kiss touches my mouth, I feel my whole body tremble.

"Goodnight, Maisie," he whispers, before he lets me go on shaky legs back to my room.

"You look beautiful," I tell her, when she finally comes down the stairs. She's kept me and Wade waiting for over half an hour, but it's worth it.

The sequin dress she's wearing is far too short, but I intend on making sure everyone at this party we're going to knows that she's mine, and anyone who wants to keep his balls swinging won't risk their eyes wandering.

"I'm worried it's too much." She pulls a face that's fuckin' adorable as she traces her fingers over the shiny sequins.

"You've clearly never been to one of Mayor Walker's parties," Wade scoffs sarcastically, placing his hat on his head and marching out the door.

He's in one hell of a bad mood, but that's hardly surprising. The fact he's even coming to this party is a bad idea. The only reason I'm going myself is because I know how much Maisie wants to be there.

It's been two nights since she told me she'd stay and help out around here, and I can feel her warming back up to me. I see it in the way she smiles at me over breakfast, and last night when I got in late, she'd delayed dinner, so we could eat together.

We've spent time talking about what she did at art school and the gallery she worked at, and I've probably bored the shit out of her by talking about the ranch and all the plans I've got for its future.

When she said goodnight, I kissed her the same way I did the night before, and it felt fucking good.

I've put a lot on her since she's been back. I need to give her some time to absorb. I'm asking far too much of her. She likes her job in L.A, and she has friends there. I can't expect her to give all that up on a whim. Which is why I need to prove to her that I'm serious, and if it takes time for her to adjust, I'll give her all the time she needs.

I drive to the mayor's house and park my truck outside next to all the fancy cars. I can't help wondering if this party is for Leia and Caleb or just another excuse for her father to show off to the town.

"It's gonna be strange being at a party where Cora ain't flashin' her smile at any man in real leather." Wade makes an uncalled-for dig as we step up to the door, and just as I'm about to stare him down, Maisie shocks me and bursts out laughing. I get her and her mom weren't close, especially after she left, but I worry about how she's handling her loss. I never had much time for my father, but his death still hit me like a freight train.

I knock on the door, and when one of the catering staff answers, we're immediately offered champagne from the tray he has resting on his hand.

Leia races straight for us and hugs Maisie, telling her how incredible she looks before she moves on to Wade and squeezes him tight. I notice the way he holds on to her for a second or two longer than he should, and I feel his pain.

A Carson man's pride will always be his downfall.

"Garrett, good to see you." Leia smiles me a fake smile, proving that she still hasn't forgiven me for trampling on her friend's heart. She moves in for a hug, clutching at the sleeves of my shirt tightly.

"Hurt her a second time, and I'll bury you on that ranch you value so much," she warns quietly into my ear before pulling away and smiling sweetly.

"You don't mind if I borrow Maisie, do you? There's some people I want her to meet."

"Not at all." I smile back at her politely and watch as she leads my girl into the lion's den.

"I need another drink." Wade downs the dregs of his champagne and grabs another from the tray that passes us, he's staring across the room to where Caleb is standing with his father and Mayor Walker.

"What does she see in him? I mean, apart from the fact he saves puppies for a livin'." It's rare to see Wade bitter, but he's given up a lot over the past twelve months, and now he's giving up hope on her, too.

"I don't know, Wade, but scowlin' at him ain't gonna change anything."

"You're forgettin' the fact he sold drugs to a rapist." He forces the words out of his tightly clamped jaw and continues to look at him.

"I don't forget shit. And I ain't the one letting him marry the woman I love." I remind him before injecting myself into the crowd of people and preparing myself to be fake for a few hours.

I talk to the mayor and the commissioner and I make nice with Ronnie Mason for the sake of all who are watching. The sly fucker makes a public display of offering his condolences to me over Cora's 'brutal' murder and asks the commissioner for an update on how the investigation's being handled. There's no denying that he thinks I'm behind it. Half the people in this room will be assuming it, too. I don't blame them for it. If I were them, I'd be thinking the same.

I distract myself from the urge I've got to hit him by

watching Maisie. She's a natural socializer, has a way of drawing people to her, and seems to instantly make them smile. I watch her talking with Joe Mason and his wife. I assume she must be complimenting Aubrey on what she's wearing when she reaches out and touches the fabric of her dress, and the smile Aubrey makes back at her looks genuine. It's rare to see Aubrey smile these days. Our moms were good friends, and we spent a lot of time together as kids. It's odd how she feels like a stranger to me now. Maisie moves on around the room with Leia, and when her 'supposed' friend leaves her alone, talking to Leonard Mason and a bunch of his friends, I decide it's time to go over and make it clear to them who she came here with.

"I brought you another drink, darlin'." I move to stand beside her, placing a fresh glass of champagne in her hand, then I curl my arm around her hip and get a kick out of the way she blushes when I kiss her cheek.

"Thank you," she smiles at me, like she has me all figured out.

"I was just telling Maisie, here, how much I miss competing against your brother." Leonard knows exactly what he's doing, he thinks my brother's a quitter, and although I can't argue with him on that fact, I still wanna punch his lights out.

"I'm sure he'll make a comeback soon enough." I look around the room, trying to locate him; I ain't seen him in a while, and come to think about it, I ain't seen Cole, either. These kinda events, us Carsons tend to suffer together.

"You like the rodeo, Maisie?" Leonard asks her, roaming his eyes over her body and not taking the look I'm giving him as a serious enough warning.

"I love the rodeo." She answers him like an excited child, oblivious to the filth he's thinking. Me however, I know exactly where his thoughts are at. He's thinking about ripping that dress off her body and fucking her, and I'm thinking about pushing his eyeballs into the back of his skull and stamping on his balls.

"You'll have to come watch sometime. It's always good to have some support in the crowd." I clutch Maisie's hip a little tighter, to stop myself from acting on those thoughts.

"I'm sure Garrett will take me soon, maybe when Wade gets back on the saddle." She answers him with a polite tone and a slither of rejection that pleases me.

"What are *they* doing here?" One of Leonard's buddies slaps him on the chest and nods toward the door that the River Boys just stepped through.

"Oh them, they're Leia's friends. I remember they were real good to her when she got her drink spiked a few years ago," Maisie answers innocently, and the look Leonard gives me assures me that he knows his younger brother was responsible for all that shit.

Leia's younger sister heads straight over to them, and I see the nod the mayor gives Noah once he's noticed they've arrived.

"Shifty fuckers, in my opinion. But then, there's lots of people in Fork River a pretty girl like you should be wary of," Leonard tells Maisie before he raises his glass to me, and when it causes her cheeks to flush pink, it escalates an anger inside me that almost has me laying him out on the mayor's fancy marble floor. And sensibly, he steps away, leading his friends across the room to join his brothers.

"Who's that man, standing with old man Mason? I recognize him." Maisie asks, looking at the tall, ugly fucker Ronnie seems to have appointed to remain by his side for protection since Cora died. I find it a little suspicious that he's taken such drastic measures. It's almost as if he's expecting to be next.

"You probably recognise him from bein' at the ranch. He used to work for us before Garrett fired his ass." Wade steps up from outta nowhere, glaring across the room to where the Masons are now gathered together.

"Why was that? He sure looks like he could be handy." Maisie laughs before taking a sip from her glass.

"You remember that day I found you in the river with Finn?" I remind her.

"Well, he was the stupid asshole who sent you into a wood full of bears and wolves without a gun."

"Yes, I remember. You can't seriously have fired him for that?" She stares at me, shocked.

"Did more than fire him," Wade pipes up again, making me want to strike him. "Tied the fucker to a tree with open wounds and left him out as a snack." He informs her with a sadistic grin, causing an expression of shock mixed with a little fear to cast over her face.

"Garrett... he's kidding, right?" Maisie looks at me with those wide, blue eyes.

"No, he ain't kiddin'." I shake my head unapologetically. I won't deny it, and I certainly ain't ashamed about it. Seth Granger is lucky to be alive after the stunt he pulled.

"Garrett, you can't *do* things like that." Maisie looks so sexy when she's agitated. She doesn't know it, but she's got the attention of every man in the room, and when she goes to strop off, I grab her firmly by the arm, then take the champagne flute out of her hand and pass it to Wade.

"What are you doing?" She struggles against my grip while trying not to make a scene, and I keep her tight to my body, smiling at those we pass as I maneuver her to the bathroom.

"Garrett. Tell me what you're doing." She growls at me like a caged tiger when I close the door and flick the lock.

"Yeah, I did that to the bastard who could have so easily got you killed, and I'd do it again. In fact, I'd do worse."

"And you just had to drag me in here, in front of all those people, to tell me that?" she fumes.

God, she's perfect when she's mad.

"No." Taking her by surprise, I move toward her and push the sequin dress from her thighs up her body. Then lifting her onto the basin unit, I press my forehead into hers.

"But I figured you'd rather us be alone when I did this…" My fingers edge beneath the seam of her panties, and I roll them off her hips so I can let my middle finger skim through her pussy lips. The way she throws her head back and moans tells me she's been as desperate for me to touch her there, as I have.

"Leonard Mason made you blush when he told you, you were pretty," I point out, slowly circling my finger against her clit, and cupping her chin in my hand, so she has to focus on me.

"The only man who's allowed to make those pretty cheeks of yours flush pink from now on is me." I drop to my knees before resting her legs over my shoulders, then I look up and watch her reaction as I replace my finger with my tongue. I admire the shock and thrill on her face and the sharp intake of breath she makes as her fingers claw at my hair, practically pulling it from the scalp. My tongue flicks against her sensitive flesh, allowing me to taste her innocent pussy. I've thought about how this might be, since the day I found her pleasuring herself on my bed all those years ago. I succumbed to temptation back then, the same way I am now. I tasted her first orgasm off her fingers that day, and I never forgot how sweet it was. Now I'm gonna taste it on my tongue. I tease her soaked entrance with my finger, pushing a little inside to test how tight she is. She thrashes her hips so desperately against my mouth and takes what she needs. Doing this in Mayor Walker's bathroom isn't exactly the way I saw it playing out, but desperation and jealousy can do strange things to a man, especially one who's as obsessed as I am. I keep my eyes on hers, watching her come apart for me and wondering how I ever got a second shot at this. Maybe God wants to give me Heaven on earth before he sends me to Hell for my sins. Right now, I don't care. I'd condemn myself to it happily, if it means I get to keep her while I'm here.

My tongue quickens its pace, and I edge my finger a little deeper inside her. And when her legs start to tremble, and her breaths become more rapid, she screams my name as she floods my tongue. I make sure I've lapped up every trace of her pleasure, before I slide my body back up hers and kiss her mouth so hard, she's forced to taste it for herself.

A loud, heavy knock at the door interrupts us, but I ignore it.

"Garrett." A male voice calls out, thumping at it again.

"I'm busy," I call back. Maisie grips at my shirt and buries her head into my chest to stifle the fit of giggles she's broken into.

"I really think you should get out here." Whoever it is sounds serious, and when I pull myself away from Maisie, I give her a chance to slide off the counter and straighten herself up before I open the door.

Sawyer looks worried when I swing it open and snarl at him.

"What the fuck is it?" I snap.

"It's Wade, he's pretty wasted. I think it's time he went home." Reaching behind me, I take Maisie's hand before I barge past him and head towards the hall, where everyone seems to have gathered around the staircase. I see my brother squaring up to Noah, who's trying to stop him from stepping up onto the middle platform where Mayor Walker is making his speech, with his daughter and her fiancé beside him. I have to let go of Maisie's hand so I can nudge through the congregation of people and get to my brother before he gets past Noah.

"So, my wife and I would like you all to raise a toast with us and Mr. Mason to congratulate the happy couple. To Leia and Caleb." Walker raises his glass, and Wade shoves Noah so hard it sends him off balance, allowing him to pass. When he steps up, he snatches the champagne glass right out of the mayor's hand.

"Yes, all you folks, raise your glasses to Caleb-fuckin'-Mason," he slurs, narrowing his eyes on the shocked-looking man who's holding Leia's hand.

"Our town's amazin' vet. A pillar of this here community, and the guy who's probably responsible for gettin' half your daughters raped." Shock and gasps echo around the room, and I push a little harder to get through the crowd so I can drag him the fuck out of here.

"Wade," I warn him when I get to the front, and I step up to pull him away.

"Leave me. I'm fine." He tries to shove me off, but I stand firm and shake my head.

"Relax, Garrett, I'm just lettin' Leia here know a little somethin' about the man she's gonna marry."

Leia stares at him with tears filling her eyes, and a disappointed look on her face. I can see how hurt she is by my brother's actions, and Wade must see it, too, when she bursts into sobs and rushes up the stairs. Caleb acts like he's fuckin' innocent by shaking his head and chasing after her.

"I think it's time you took your brother home." Mayor Walker looks at me with a furious glint in his eyes. Of all the enemies you could make in this town, he's the last one you'd want. He's powerful, and he has guys like the River Boys on his payroll for a reason.

"I second that." Old man Mason steps up from behind him

and scowls at me like I'm a piece of shit, and I decide he's been getting far too big for his boots lately.

Seth puffs out his chest like he's about to do something, knowing that half the town is here as witnesses. I decide my only option is to back down.

"Come on, Wade," I whisper to my brother, somehow managing to stay calm. He's still looking up the stairs where Leia ran and seems to have lost all his fight, and he doesn't struggle when I tug him off the step where he's standing. He keeps staring at that empty space as I walk him through the silent crowd, take Maisie's hand in my free one, and then lead them back to the truck.

No one speaks on the journey home, and I don't feel a single shred of jealousy when Maisie takes my brother's hand in hers and rests her head on his shoulder instead of mine.

All I got for him is sympathy.

CHAPTER 9

MAISIE

I wake up to the sound of bustling out in the yard. Last night when we got home, I got the sense that Garrett wanted to speak to his brother alone, so I took myself to bed with happy thoughts of what he did to me in the bathroom before we were interrupted.

I find Garrett in his office, he's dressed in jeans and a tight tee and looks ready to get to work outside, yet he's leaning over the desk staring at the computer screen in front of him with a frustrated look on his face.

"Guess I missed breakfast, huh?" I step inside and move over to see what's got him looking so agitated.

"I saved ya some. Perks of dating the boss," he smirks.

"Dating? I don't recall us going on a single date," I point out.

"We've been on plenty. I took ya to Cahoots when you first arrived in town. I took you to the rodeo, and I'm pretty sure we attended that party last night, together."

"I can assure you that none of those class as dates. First, and only time, you ever took me to Cahoots was with Wade, and you ignored me all night, *and* ended up knocking out some guy. The rodeo, you left me in Columbus…"

"And came back for ya" he interrupts, defensively.

"And knocked out *another* guy." I place my hands on my hips and look up at him.

"He deserved it. They both did." He shows no remorse, and I guess I can't argue that. Jason was the guy responsible for breaking in and causing his Pops to have a heart attack.

"And last night?" I question, interested to hear how he considers an engagement party, that ended in disaster, a date.

"I'd rather not talk about last night, and I'm sure Wade feels the same." Garrett looks disappointed.

"You know I'm gonna have to call Leia, and check she's okay? It was pretty sucky of me not to do that last night, and if I'm honest with you, as bad as I feel for Wade and what he's going through, I haven't got much of an excuse for what he did."

"Ya don't need to make excuses for him; just do right by ya friend," he tells me with a sad smile.

"What were you focusing so hard on?" I change the subject and get back to looking at the screen.

"All this shit. Ya mom liked to take care of it, guess it was her way of making sure we didn't cut her out of anything, and although I ain't got too much good to say about her, she was good at keeping things handled."

"You trusted my mom with the finances?" I check I'm hearing him right.

"Hell no! The ranch has an accountant, and I have a separate one who I was paying, personally, to scrutinize everything. But there's a lot of day-to-day shit that needs takin' care of. Bills need to be paid, payments need chasin' up, and Cora always was good at chasin' money." He looks guilty for what he just said, and I put him at ease by laughing a little.

"Getting Cora to do the day-to-day admin kept her out of our way. I appreciate ya saying you'll help, but if it gets too much, I can employ someone to take care of it."

"Go play with some horses." I take his hat off the table and place it on his head, before I bump him out of the way with my hip and make myself comfortable in his leather desk chair.

"I mean it, this ain't what I'm offering. I wanna give you more than an office job." I hate that he thinks this is a burden to me. I want to make things easier around here. The more time Garrett spends on the ranch, the more likely it is that Wade can get back to doing what he loves.

"I can take care of this, I'm always chasing up sales for the gallery. Let me help."

Garrett kisses my cheek as I start scrolling through the spreadsheet and figuring the system. I've seen more and more of his playful side come out since I've been back, and I like it a lot.

"I'll have Josie bring ya breakfast in here," he tells me, as he heads out the door.

"And a coffee. Black," I call out after him.

"When did you become a woman, Maisie Wildman?" I look up and find him staring at me from the doorframe.

I want to tell him it was the day he broke my heart, but I also don't wanna kill his vibe.

"I'm still waiting for you to make me one, Garrett Carson." I throw him a seductive look and watch the smirk on his face turn to shock, before he shakes his head and leaves me to it.

I spend most of the morning working on the spreadsheet, and figuring out what payments need to be chased up.

I find time to call Leia and check she's okay, and although I can tell how pissed she is at Wade for ruining her big night, I can tell by the tone of her voice that she'll forgive him for it. Not without making him suffer, though, I'm sure.

Garrett comes in for lunch, but there's no sign of Wade. Apparently, he rode off to one of the line camps to check for any stragglers, and I hope he doesn't hide himself away for too long.

Me and Garrett are just finishing up the subs that Josie made us for lunch, when Finn knocks at the office door.

"Sorry to interrupt ya, boss." He turns his attention to me and nods his head. "Maisie." He smiles before continuing. "Sheriff Nelson's here to see ya." He looks cautiously at Garrett, who sits himself up a little straighter in the chair he's sitting in, on the other side of the desk.

"Better show him in then." He wipes his mouth with the paper napkin before screwing it up and tossing it at his plate.

A bald-headed man with dark skin steps into the room. He's big and must stand at nearly 7ft tall, but his kind face counteracts the intimidation of his size.

"Sherriff, this is Miss Wildman." Garrett introduces us.

"We spoke on the phone; you called me the night my mother died." I lean over the desk and offer him my hand.

"Yes, I remember. I'm sorry for your loss, and you can rest assured we're doing all we can to find out who is responsible," he tells me, suddenly making me feel guilty for abandoning my mission to do the same.

"Maybe we should have this conversation somewhere more private." He looks awkwardly between me and Garrett.

"No need. You can say whatever it is you have to say in front of her." Garrett sits back down and leans back in his chair casually.

"Ok," Sheriff Nelson shrugs. "I came here to give you a heads up as to where this investigation is going."

"My alibi's solid." Garrett sounds arrogantly confident.

"Yes, Miss Murphy's statement and the CCTV footage of you at the bar confirm it." He nods, and I throw a look at

Garrett and try not to make it look like I care about the fact he was with a woman, at a bar, the night my mom was killed.

"Wade was with Leia Walker all night, according to her statement. But I got no accountability for your other brother. Due to the nature of the crime and the motive he's got, Investigator Swann is looking at him as a person of interest.

"Shit." Garrett drops that cool exterior he's been putting on and scrubs his fingers over his stubble.

"Garrett, you know I got your back, but this goes over my head, and Cole ain't helping himself by refusing to cooperate. They're building a case and it's only gonna be a matter of time before they make an arrest," he warns.

"I'll speak to him," Garrett assures the sheriff. "And I appreciate ya comin' over with the heads up."

"No bother. Something sure smells good in that kitchen of yours." He changes the subject.

"Steak subs, Josie makes the bread from scratch," I tell him. I can see Garrett is worried, so I attempt to lighten the mood.

"Why don'tcha head on in there and get her to rustle ya one up?" Garrett suggests, snapping himself out of his thoughts.

"I might just do that. It's always a pleasure to see that smile of hers." Sheriff Nelson puts his hat back in place, before he heads out the door. And Garrett spins back around in his chair, looking concerned.

"Miss Murphy, huh?" I raise my eyebrows and inwardly curse myself for biting so quickly.

"She's a vet, who specializes in horses, got herself a practice over in Columbus."

"And do you meet with *all* of your vets in bars?" I ask, straightening my back and avoiding eye contact by looking at the screen in front of me.

"You're jealous," he accuses me, and when I glance back at him and see him smiling, I want to punch his handsome face.

"I am not jealous."

"Bull shit. Ya skin's practically turned green." He gets up from his chair and moves around his desk to stand beside me, resting his ass on its surface and crossing his arms.

"Unlike some people, Garrett, I don't get jealous." I shake my head and try to get back to work.

"That's good to hear because Miss Murphy is a very attractive woman, and I like to work as closely as I can with her."

I stand up, about to slap him, but he catches my wrist too quickly.

"You are fuckin' irresistible when ya get mad." He lunges forward and bites at my lip, causing my pussy to clench.

"I wasn't m..."

"I'm sure Miss Murphy appeals to plenty, but not to me," he assures me, clasping my jaw in his hand and gently kissing me where he just bit.

"I wanted to take ya out ridin' this afternoon, but I gotta go find Cole and talk some sense into him. I'll have Dalton take ya instead, if ya still wanna get out of here."

"I'd rather wait for you," I tell him, trying not to make that stupid, dreamy smile I know he brings out of me.

"Good answer." He kisses me one more time before he leaves.

CHAPTER 10

GARRETT

I wait in the diner for Cole to show up, watching the town folk come and go outside from the window. Zayne's old man runs the garage across the street, so it's a regular hang-out for the River Boys, and I can see them working on the old truck Sawyer rides around in. It reminds me that I should check in on Shelby West. The stubborn, old goat is a nightmare when it comes to asking for help, and although she's got a strapping grandson and friends that would do anything for her, none of them are ranchers. I'll have to go check in on her.

"I just wanted to say that if you did kill her, I wouldn't blame ya for it." Dolores lands my coffee in front of me, spilling it over the sides and onto the table.

"I didn't kill her." I shake my head, picking up some paper napkins to clean up the mess.

"Well, someone did, and I'd rest much better in my bed at night if I knew that someone was you." She chuckles to herself all the way back to her kitchen, and when the bell above the door chimes and my brother steps in, I can tell straight away that he's in a bad mood.

"Take it ya heard what happened at the party last night?" I ask as he takes a seat in the booth opposite me.

"Jesus Christ, Garrett, as if shit ain't hard enough for me over there. It's all I've fuckin' heard about since I woke up."

Cole holds his hand up to Dolores, who gets straight to work making his usual.

"Is this why you wanted to see me? Because I think urgent was a bit of an exaggeration."

"Trust me, Wade kickin' up dust at a party is the least of your troubles right now. I had a visit from Sheriff Nelson this mornin'. He told me Swann is makin' you a person of interest." I lower my voice as Dolores serves Cole his coffee, gossip spreads fast in this town, and Dolores is one of the main sources.

"I told you and the police where I was that night. I took a drive by myself to clear my head."

"That ain't good enough, Cole. And we both know it ain't the truth. Joe Mason was outta town that night, and I gotta real heavy suspicion that you were with his wife."

"You watch your fuckin' mouth." Cole leans across the table and speaks through his teeth at me.

"I won't have ya go to jail for a crime ya didn't commit," I warn him sternly, staring down my nose at the finger he's got pointed at my face.

"The police will get to the bottom of it. You keep her out of it,"

"You got a motive," I point out.

"We all got a motive, Garrett."

"Yeah, but we also got alibis. Shit's comin' your way, Cole. I'm just doing my duty as your brother to warn you about it." I leave a ten-dollar bill on the table and stand up, ready to leave.

"If shit got real and I brought her home, would ya support us? I know you said you would before, but a lot's changed since then. Things are bad enough between us and the Masons. I know that old fucker only employs me because he gets a kick out of bein' able to tell me what to do. If I can convince her to leave with me, it'll start a war," he asks before I have the chance to leave. I lean down and tap his chest where his shirt covers his brand.

"I can't believe that's even a fuckin' question," I whisper, tipping my hat to Dolores on my way out the door.

When I get back to the ranch, Wade is in the corral working on the horse he's trying to break, and Maisie is sitting on the fence looking mesmerized as she watches him. I head on over, leaning to rest my arms over the top rail beside her.

"You speak to Cole?" she asks, sheltering her eyes from the sun as she continues to watch Wade.

"Yep, not that it did any good." I light up a cigarette and chuckle at the way my brother's getting thrown around like a rag doll.

"Can't you just get someone from here to say they were with him? Everyone seems to do what you say," she suggests, looking so carefree with the slight breeze blowing through her hair. She doesn't seem to have a worry in the world right now, which is exactly how it should be.

"This ranch and the bunkhouse was the first place the officers looked into. All the bunkhouse boys have given their statements, none mentionin' Cole. He can't admit who he was really with that night, and the consequences of that could very well be the reason he gets accused of your mom's murder." I admit, trying my best not to sound too disheartened. I don't want my troubles bringing her down.

"Aubrey Mason?" Maisie asks casually.

"How did you know?" I stare up at her. For a girl who hasn't been in town very long, she sure has it figured.

"Leia and I talk, she told me about the history, and I see no other logical reason why Cole would want to work on the Mason ranch."

"You take that to the grave with ya," I warn her.

"Or he'll take it to his?" She looks at me questioningly. "He should own his shit, just like your other brother should," her head gestures to Wade, who's just been thrown off but is already back on the saddle.

"To be fair, Wade did some ownin' last night," I point out.

"I wouldn't call what Wade did, owning the situation." She lifts her legs back over the fence, turning her body to sit and face mine, and I position myself between her legs.

"You Carson brothers make shit real complicated," she tells me.

"Wade should be with Leia, and he should be competing. Cole should be with Aubrey, it's that simple," she explains.

"And what about me?" I ask her, creasing my brow and wondering what she's thinking.

"You're exactly where you should be." She lifts the hat off my head and places it on her own before she kisses me.

I pace the porch while I wait for her. When I see her car pull up and realize she ain't smiling, I know there's something wrong. We haven't met here since the night Cora died, and seeing her on the ranch every day without being able to touch her has driven me crazy.

"Had trouble getting away?" I go to her, checking the open fields around us before I pull her closer and kiss her lips.

It's remote enough out here at the abandoned ranch where we meet, but I also know how close an eye Joe keeps on his wife.

"Let's get inside." Aubrey checks over her shoulder before offering me a sad smile and moving around me to step through the door.

When we get inside, I don't give her a chance to talk; it's been too long since I've had her to myself. I slide my hand behind her head and kiss her lips like I've been starved of 'em.

"Cole." She pushes hard on my chest, forcing me away.

"Is this about the shit Wade pulled last night with Joe's brother, because if it is...?"

"This has to stop." She's got a serious-as-death expression on her face and looks like she's about to cry.

"You know that ain't an option." I shake my head, wondering what's gotten into her. For more than eighteen months, we've been stealing moments like this, coming out here to the old Steanman's ranch so we can be together. Old man Mason's spent a lot of money buying land and finishing off the smaller ranches. This is one of them. It's been empty for years and far enough off the grid to guarantee we won't be disturbed.

"Don't make this hard." She closes her eyes and steadies her breath before putting some space between us.

"I ain't makin' it hard, Aubrey. I ain't lettin' it happen at all." It feels like I just got her back, and there ain't no way in hell things can go back to the way they were.

"What we're doing is wrong. I'm married." When she opens her eyes back up, they're pleading with me, but I haven't come this far to start taking steps back.

"You *love* me," I remind her, grabbing her face in my hands to make sure she listens. I get that she's scared. I just don't know what she's scared of.

"It's not who I'm in love with that matters; it's who I'm married to that does." She sounds like a different woman to the one I made love to on the couch by the fire a few weeks ago. She sounds weak, and I really fucking hate it.

"A piece of paper sayin' you took his name don't mean a thing. What *we* have..."

"He wants us to start trying." She forces the words out her mouth, and they hit me in the guts like a stampede.

"Are ya fuckin' insane? Ain't it bad enough that you're stuck in hell, you wanna drag a kid into that shit, too?" I shouldn't shout at her, Aubrey's always been sensitive, but I'm angry, and I'm hurting. Over the past eighteen months these encounters have been what I've lived for.

"There's no need to be cruel." I hate the look she gives me, and I hate the way it makes me feel.

"Life's cruel, Aubrey. I learned that the day you married a Mason."

"You never asked me to marry you." She speaks bitterly. I think it's the first time in all the years that I've known her that I've heard her take that kinda tone. Aubrey's soft and gentle. She's sweet and kind. She's everything I ain't.

"Don't pretend there ain't more to it than that." I shake my head, and march to the door to stop her leaving through it.

"Move out my way, Cole." She stares past me like she's scared to look into my eyes.

"Not until you tell me why." I continue to block her.

"You promised you'd never ask me." She keeps that stern look on her face, and it doesn't suit her. Something is not right.

"Yeah, well, I'm askin' now. If you're gonna break my heart again, I need to know the reason why."

"When we started this, you told me you didn't have a heart to break," she reminds me when her eyes find mine again.

"Well, I found out that I did." I hold her stare, and when it doesn't look like she's gonna give in, I kiss her again.

I hope it reminds her why we started this and puts some sense back in her head.

"It's only gonna make it harder," she tells me, but she doesn't pull away, so I ignore her, lifting her up and carrying her over to the table.

"Tell me to stop." I raise the long skirt she's wearing and take my cock out of my jeans. Edging it towards her, I hook my finger into her panties and drag them to one side, clearing a path for me to enter her. She grabs the front of my shirt, and instead of pushing me back, she lies down on the table's surface and drags me down with her. I push inside her, taking both her hands in mine, squeezing them tight and using them to pin her to the table.

While she uses her eyes to pin me, they anchor on to my soul and bleed all their pain into my chest. I'll never know why she chose him, and she told me a long time ago that she'll never leave him. She promises me it's not because she loves him. She tells me she wishes things could be different, and I know from the way she gives me her body that she means it. When we're alone together, we shut out the world, and she gives me everything that should be mine. The only thing she doesn't give me is answers. It frustrates me, but those were her conditions, and if I get to have her even just a little bit, it's a small price to pay.

Aubrey likes me to look at her when I fuck her, and I often wonder if Joe does the same. I wonder if he makes her cum the same way I do, and I wonder if he holds her after. See, that's the difference between me and my brothers, we're all dark in our own ways, but Garrett and Wade can be dragged into the light. Me, I clutch at the shadows. I like to hurt inside and out. I welcome pain, and there ain't nothing more painful than imagining him and her together.

I pick up my pace, thrusting into her so hard the table starts to move across the room, and the sweet, innocent woman I've been in love with my whole life looks up at me, daring me to fuck her harder.

This is the woman I keep in my head when we're apart. A woman who, when we're alone, allows herself to fall into the dark with me.

Out there, she has to be perfect, she stands to heel like a puppy, but here with me, she can be whoever she wants to be. She can be the teenage girl who gave her heart to a boy who didn't deserve it. She can be the poor, tragic housewife who tried to move on but never let that boy go. Or she can be the whore, who fucks her husband's ranch hand.

All I've ever really wanted her to be is mine.

It's *my* name she screams when the orgasm hits her, and the tears she cries are for me, too, because she doesn't want this to be the end of us either.

I pull out my cock before I come and drag her off the table on to her knees, taking her head in my hands and fucking her mouth so I can finish inside there. Tonight, when that Mason cunt kisses her goodnight, she can think about me while he's doing it. Her fingers grip onto the waist of my jeans as I pull out from between her lips, and when she looks up at me, she looks like she's praying.

"I know you don't understand, but I need you to forgive me. I can't have you hate me." The tears are streaming down her cheeks, and seeing her hurting makes me want to scoop her up and absorb all her pain. It even makes me wanna cry a little myself. But I don't. I can't recall ever crying. Not when my mama left or when Breanna killed herself. I certainly didn't shed no tears when Pops died.

"I could never hate you." I frown and shake my head back at her. That, right there, is the problem. If I could hate this woman, maybe I could heal. There's so much hate inside me, that some days I think I'll go up in flames from it. But none of it's for her. Aubrey owns the tiny fragment of my soul that's still intact. It's the part of me that allows me to walk away from her and trust that she knows what she's doing. And on the nights when I've thought about making everything end for good, it's what's kept me alive.

I've often wondered if the choices she made had something to do with the accident. Things were never the same for her after she lost her friend when we were younger. They were never the same for us, either.

Aubrey was in the car the night her friend was killed. She wasn't even the one driving, but I don't think she's ever forgiven herself for surviving. I tried to get her through, tried to make her speak to someone, but she wouldn't let me, she shut me out. And that's how I lost her.

It makes no sense, but I swear her marrying Joe Mason was

her punishing herself for not dying in that car, too.

"Don't do it." I raise her back up onto her feet, and I don't care how weak I sound. "You don't want this; you won't be happy."

"I can try to be without this reminding me of how it could have been," she whispers, sliding the pad of her thumb over my bottom lip so tenderly it makes my heart stop.

"Come back to Copper Ridge with me. Tell me what you're scared of, and I'll fix it," I whisper, letting her see all the hurt inside me and hoping she takes pity on me.

"You can't fix it, Cole." More tears run down her cheeks, and I swallow the lump wedged in my throat.

"Watch me." I plead for her to trust me, and when she smiles, it ain't a happy one.

"We gotta grow up, Cole. Make the best of the lives we got. I want you to leave the ranch. I can't move on when I see you every day." Any softness I had inside me turned to stone.

"You ain't supposed to move on. You're supposed to do what ya heart tells you," I growl at her.

"And is this what your heart's telling *you* to do? Fuck someone else's wife?" The sting of her words and the spite in her eyes make me wanna throw my fist at the wall. "I'm his, Cole. We both gotta accept that." When she goes to push past me, I grab her arm and drag her back, and she shocks the hell out of me when she spins around and slaps my face.

"If you really love me, you'll do this for me." Her lips are trembling, and her eyes are drowning in sadness.

"Don't do this to me," I beg her.

"I'm sorry." She tugs her wrist from my grip and walks away, getting in her car and starting up the engine. I'm too weak to chase after her, I'm too weak to even stay standing, and as I drop my ass onto the porch step and watch her drive away, I feel that last fragment of good in my soul leave with her.

I lie in bed listening to the rain on the roof and watching it pelt against the window, and I think about the night Bill Carson died and how I waited for Garrett to come home.

I found out that night what kinda man Garrett was. The kind I should be running from, but as I lie here, knowing that he's in the room next to me alone, all I can think about is running *to* him.

I get out of bed and open my door, stepping across the hall and quietly opening his door to let myself inside. I can't tell if he's awake or asleep because he's rolled on his side facing his window, but I creep closer, lifting the covers and sliding in behind him anyway. I let my fingers trace over his strong, broad shoulder, and when he turns around, and his eyes meet mine, I smile at him.

"Hey," I whisper, and when he shifts the rest of his body to face mine, he takes my face in his hands and kisses my lips so softly I swear I feel my body float off the bed. He tucks one of his arms around my back and pulls me tighter to his body. I rest my head on his chest, and as he strokes his hand through my hair, I notice the bumpy scar on his chest. I've seen the symbol enough times to know what it is, and I watched him branding the calves a few days ago with the same mark.

"I've only ever wanted it to be you," I admit, finding it so

69

much easier to say without looking at him. It's dark in here, all we have is the moonlight, but when he forces my head to face him, I see the confused look on his face.

"Why?" he asks in a low, raspy tone that spreads warmth across my chest.

"I feel safe with you. I feel like I belong to you in some kinda way. You're gonna think I'm crazy, but I've felt it since that first time you looked at me out on the porch. And I like it. I like how it feels." I move my body so I'm straddling his hips, and Garrett's eyes don't fall from mine. Not even when I pull the tee I'm wearing up over my head and expose the top half of my body to him. All I'm wearing now is a tiny pair of cotton panties, and I can feel myself soaking through them, knowing that his cock is so close. It's hard to explain how it's possible to desire something I've never had, and it doesn't matter how many times I've imagined this moment, I'm still nervous.

I take Garrett's hand in mine and guide it up to touch me, and when his huge, rough palm cups over one of my tits, he squeezes gently and narrows his eyes at me.

"I don't want to wait anymore. We've waited long enough," I tell him, and when he sits up on the bed so his body presses against mine, he reaches behind me, takes a handful of my hair and kisses me so hard I lose my breath.

"That warning I gave you before I let you go, I meant it. If I have you, ain't nothin' in this world is gonna stop me from keeping you," he warns, and all I can do is nod back at him. I know what he's saying is true, and I like the sound of it. Garrett returns my nod, and the hand he still has on my chest slides up to rest around my throat when he kisses me again. There's a possessiveness to his touch, yet it remains soft, and when he rolls our bodies so I'm back on the mattress and he's above me, his kisses start to lower.

I look up at his ceiling and brace myself for what's coming

as his lips press against my skin, making a slow trail all the way down my body until he reaches my panties and when he looks up at me with those deliciously dark eyes, I crave to feel his mouth there again. He peels the fabric off my hips and tosses them over his shoulder before he gives me exactly what I need. Only this time, it's different. He kisses me there the same way he kissed my mouth, and I have to reach back and grip hold of his headboard to sustain the ache of what it builds inside me.

I feel myself edging closer, my hips start to buck against his mouth, and that's when he pulls away. Crawling back up my body, he slides the sweatpants he's wearing off his hips, so his hard, heavy cock rests between my legs.

It feels so big, and when I look up at him, and his dark hair has fallen over his face, everything suddenly feels intense. I reach my hand up, pushing the hair out of his eyes, and he kisses my wrist. It's such a tiny simple gesture, but it makes my pulse beat faster and the butterflies in my stomach flutter.

"You scared?" he whispers, and I nod my head at him because it seems pointless lying.

"You got no reason to be scared." I look down between us and beg to differ, but I take a deep breath and smile to let him know I'm ready. His hand slides down my thigh and reaches around to my ass, slightly lifting my leg so he can fit better between my legs, and when I feel the tip of his cock brush against me, I gasp.

"It's gonna have to hurt a little first, but it won't last," he promises, slowly rocking his hips so his thick cock slips between my pussy lips. It feels so good that it relieves some of the tension. He moves with such ease, making me slicker, and when my body starts to relax again and I look up at him, he's staring right back at me, holding my gaze as he gradually pushes himself inside me.

I hold my breath and squeeze the top of his arms when the pressure starts to get uncomfortable.

"Breathe," Garrett reminds me, taking my jaw in his hand and holding it tight. I take a deep one and nod to let him know I'm ready for him to continue, and I feel the tension in his fingers tighten a little more as his cock continues to stretch me.

"You're perfect, Maisie Wildman," he tells me, shaking his head like there's something about this he doesn't understand. It distracts me from the pain, and when he pulls my head up to meet his lips and gives me the rest of him, I moan into his mouth and feel that grip he's got on me crush harder.

"Holy fuck," he growls, holding himself inside me for a few seconds before he carefully eases back and then pushes again. I lift my arms, and wrap them around his neck, rocking my hips against his. He's gentle, soft, and all the things I used to think he was incapable of.

"Is it hurtin'?" he asks, lifting his head from where he's been watching himself push inside me.

"A little," I admit and see the guilt in his eyes.

"I'll fix it," he promises. Taking two of his fingers, he sucks them into his mouth, dropping them between my legs and circling them against my clit.

It doesn't take the pain away, but it gives it a new edge, and it doesn't take long for my hips to start thrusting up at him, craving for more of it.

I'm a sick fuck for the pleasure I'm taking out of her suffering but being inside her and feeling my cock stretch her pussy to be my perfect fit feels too good. I try to make it as comfortable as possible, but I know she's hurting, and I wish I could take that part away for her. I meant what I said before, Maisie Wildman has no reason to be scared anymore. She's mine. Mine to care for. Mine to keep safe, and mine to love.

I was never really sure what that would feel like, but I feel it now as I watch her give all her innocence to me.

I've never wanted anything more in my life than I do her, not even this ranch.

"Come for me," I tell her, applying more pressure to my fingers and thrusting inside her a little faster. I can feel myself getting close, and I won't finish until she experiences how good this can be. Her pussy clasps at my cock like a vice. One I never want to be released from, and when her cheeks flush red, and her breaths start to quicken, I admire the way she looks as she comes all over my cock. The tension in my body cripples me as I offload inside her freshly broken pussy and try my best not to crush her jaw with my hand.

I slide my hand over the sweat on her skin and steady the tremble of her thighs by pressing them tighter against my hips, and when she looks up at me and smiles, I feel as evil as the devil himself for wanting to take her all over again.

"D'ya feel like a woman now?" I decide I want to make her laugh, too, and when it works, she clenches her face up like it caused her pain and reminds me that my cock's still inside her.

Steadily I pull out, wrapping her up in my arms and lying beside her.

"I feel a lot of things right now," she answers my question, looking up at me with a beautiful spark in her eyes.

"You realize your room just became vacant, right? You ain't sleepin' anywhere but here from now on."

"Sounds good to me," her dainty fingers trace over the hair on my chest and around the brand I'm marked with.

"What is it?" she asks sleepily. "And don't say it's nothing, no secrets, remember?"

"It ain't nothin'. It's important," I admit, thinking back to the night when I took it; every single man that was there, and did the same, hasn't let me down since.

"It's a promise."

"Kinda like a sacred vow?" She somehow manages to yawn and talk at the same time.

"Exactly like that. It's what's gonna make sure this place is still standin' long after we're gone." I watch her fingers soften over my bumpy, scarred flesh and when her body becomes heavier and her breaths deepen, I reach for the cover and pull it back over us, and fall asleep myself.

I wake up in bed all by myself and hope I didn't dream what happened last night.

"Morning, cowboy." I hear Maisie's voice and lift my head

off the pillow, scrubbing my face to take the harshness of the sun out of my eyes.

"You missed breakfast," she smirks, moving from the door towards the bed and placing a tray on my lap.

"What time is it?" I ask, wondering how the hell I managed to sleep past breakfast.

"Just gone eight," she tells me, heading over to the window and looking out across the yard. "And you won't believe it, but everyone seems to be functioning without you." She has a clever grin on her face when she looks back at me.

"Come here." I place the tray on my bedside table and reach across the bed to grab her waist and drag her back into it. I start to kiss her, but she wriggles out of my arms and holds me back.

"You're taking a day off today," she informs me, slamming her hand over my mouth to stop me from arguing. "And that's the last time we have sex without using protection. Mrs. Edwards' toes would curl if she knew what we did last night."

"Who the fuck is Mrs. Edwards?" I question her.

"My sex ed teacher. She taught me how to put a rubber on a banana, and last night I'm pretty sure I failed my first exam." She looks like she's thinking seriously now, and I quickly intervene before she lets it ruin her mood.

"Don't worry about that shit; I'll take care of it," I promise, leaning forward and making sure I get that kiss I've been wanting since I opened my eyes.

She doesn't seem to question me, which pleases me, and when she forces me to lay back on the bed by crawling on top of me, I brush the long, blonde hair back off her face, tuck it behind her ear and take a few seconds to study her face.

"You look like you're about to say something philosophical," she laughs at me, and I lick my lips and taste a trace of the syrup she must have had on her pancakes before she came up.

"Come on, I wanna show ya something." I leap out of bed and pull on my sweatpants, taking her hand and dragging her down the stairs. I forget that Maisie's only wearing one of my shirts and a pair of panties until I spot the look on Dalton's face as I rush us across the yard.

"You wanna keep them eyeballs in their sockets, you'll take 'em off my girl," I warn him as we pass and when we get to it, I open up the door to the huge barn.

"What are you doing?" Maisie giggles as I drag her inside and lead her up the stairs. I place both my hands over her eyes, and when she reaches for a bannister, it reminds me that I need to get one fixed.

I manage to get her to the top of the stairs, and when I pull my hands away, I step to the side so I can see the look on her face.

Seeing it makes all the hours I spent out here, clearing the place out and fixing it up, worth it.

"Garrett?" She looks around the loft space that I've converted into a studio for her with a shocked smile on her face, one that makes all the agony I felt when I thought I'd never get her back worth it, too.

"If there's anythin' ya don't like, I can change it, and if the lightning ain't right, I can have Tate figure something out; he's good with electrics."

"It's perfect." She still looks taken aback as she heads over to the easel that's placed beside the loft door, reminding me to show her why this is the space I chose.

"This ain't the best part," I tell her, shifting the bolt on the door and sliding it open so she can see for herself.

Her mouth drops open, and tears, that I assume are happy ones, fill her eyes as she stares out at the view.

"I figure all artists need a good backdrop." I step up behind her and wrap my arms around her waist, resting my chin on her shoulder and enjoying the view with her. From here, all you can see are open fields and the mountains that close them in. There will be gorgeous sunsets and stunning sunrises if I ever let her out of bed early enough to see one.

"I get it." She angles her head to look up at me, and I furrow my brow and try and understand what she means.

"I get why you fight so hard for this. It's heaven on earth. I didn't see that when I first came here, but I see it now." She spins her body in my arms and wraps her arms around my neck. "I'm only young. But I know what I want, and I want to be here with you, forever," she tells me. I lift her up in my arms and carry her over to the couch that I had Wade help me haul up here, so she could sit and appreciate the view while she takes her breaks, and I hope to God that she ain't too sore because I'm about to show the girl what forever's gonna feel like.

I sit at the table opposite Wade, waiting for Maisie to come down from her shower, and he stares back at me like he's expecting me to say something.

"Out with it," he breathes out heavily, tapping his fingers on the table.

"This ain't you," I tell him straight up, no bullshit. He's avoided me since the night of Leia Walker's party; in fact he's avoided everyone.

"I don't think you're in the position to be telling someone they ain't who they are right now." He raises his eyebrow and gives me a judgemental glare. "It's freaky how much you're smiling."

"It's amazing what can happen to a man when he swallows his pride," I advise him, and the cold stare he gives me back tells me he won't be swallowing his anytime soon.

"If you ain't gonna do anythin' about the Leia issue, you're gonna need a different focus. You need to get back to doin' what you love, Wade," I tell him seriously. I know he's stuck around here for her, but I also know he's done it for me, too.

"It ain't that easy. You need me here."

"I'll figure it out. I'll hire more help; I got Maisie helping out with the paperwork so I can get back out there more, too."

"Garrett, you just got the woman you've been pining over for three years back; you wanna be makin' up for lost time, not workin' ya ass into the ground. You took the flack around here for years when Pops was still alive. I had my fun. Maybe it's time for me to grow up and take some of that flack for you." He strokes his hand over his mouth and stares at the table.

"I won't let that happen. You're gonna do what makes you happy, and if you ain't gonna grab your balls and tell Leia Walker how you feel before she marries that son of a bitch, you're gonna get back on the broncs. I'm head of this family, and that's an order," I snigger at him, despite being very fuckin' serious, and when Maisie steps into the room, I can tell from the look on her face that she's nervous about what she's got to say.

"Can I get a ride somewhere?" she asks sweetly, twisting on her heels and fluttering her lashes at me, confirming my suspicions that I ain't gonna like what follows.

"Where to darlin'?" I stand up and make my way over to her.

"The Mason Ranch." She looks up at me and grins.

"Good luck with that one." Wade taps me on the shoulder and uses this as an excuse to cut our conversation short.

"And why would ya wanna go there?" I question her, trying not to show how pissed I am at the thought of it.

"Well, I forgot, what with all the stuff happening between us and the bathroom incident, but Aubrey Mason invited me and Leia over to her place for lunch today. Leia needs me to go to make it less awkward." She waits for my response, and when I don't give her one, she shakes her head.

"You know what, it's a silly idea. I'll just call Leia and tell her she should go by herself." When she goes to walk away I grab her arm and drag her back. I'm always hearing folk say relationships are about compromise. Maisie's a firecracker; it's one of the things I fell in love with her for. I don't want her to change and become a weak, broken-down woman like Aubrey Mason.

"I'll take ya," I tell her, and when she squeals and lands a kiss on my cheek I can't help but smile. I get Wade's point, about it being scary. I've never been much of a smiler, but then, I've never had much to smile about.

"Just be on your guard; the Masons ain't nice people, they may seem it, but they ain't."

"Aubrey seems harmless enough." Maisie looks at me like I'm being overcautious. I probably am, but when it comes to her, I always will be.

"Aubrey's a good person. It will be nice for her to have a friend," I tell her, tamping down all the things I really wanna say. "Just don't get too involved."

"Cross my heart." She reaches up on her toes to kiss me again before I grab my hat and let her lead me out to the truck.

CHAPTER 14

MAISIE

Since I was the one who came up with the 'no secret' rule, I feel guilty for lying to Garrett as he pulls up outside Joe and Aubrey Mason's home. It's much smaller than the main house, and seeing as it's right opposite the bunkhouse, I wonder if I'll see Cole.

"Call when you need pickin' up," Garrett tells me when I lean across the console to kiss him before I get out.

"I'm sure you got better things to do than run around after me," I tell him, reminding myself that what I'm doing here is for the good of the whole Carson family.

"Can't think of anythin'." He shakes his head, and it makes me smile. "Enjoy your lunch and remember what I said," he warns before pulling away, and I can tell that he ain't happy about leaving me here.

I straighten myself out and make my way toward the front door. I've got no idea how Aubrey is gonna respond to my visit. What I told Garrett about her inviting me here was a complete lie, but I know it's the only way I'd get to see her by myself. I knock on the door, hoping that she's in because I'm gonna look pretty stupid if I have to call Garrett back to fetch me because Aubrey isn't here.

The door opens, and she looks shocked to see me.

"Hey, my name's Maisie. We got introduced at the party

the other night." I smile warmly, but the worried look on her face doesn't falter.

"I remember you. You're Garrett Carson's girl, right?"

"Yeah." I nod my head, liking the way that sounds a hell of a lot.

"Can I come in? There's something I want to talk to you about." I watch her back away from the door and open it a little wider, and when I step inside, I'm a little taken aback by how basic it is. Everyone knows the Masons have money, so I'm surprised that there's not even a television in here.

"What can I help you with?" she asks me curiously, heading over to the kitchen and placing a kettle on the stove.

"I don't wanna make this awkward, but I know who Cole was with the night my mom got killed."

"How'd ya know that?" she snaps, the worry on her face giving her away, too.

"Well, I didn't for sure, until you just reacted that way, but I was pretty confident about it before I came here." The woman closes her eyes as if she's about to cry, but somehow she holds it together.

"I don't know what you're thinking, but.."

"It ain't important what I think. What's important is that Cole doesn't go to jail for something he didn't do. He's refusing to tell the police he was with you. He's got no other alibi and plenty of reasons why he'd want my mom dead. I don't know you, and I know this is asking a lot. I can imagine the trouble it could get you into. But those Carson brothers have lost so much. I can't let them lose each other ,too."

Aubrey takes a seat and covers her face with her hands.

"Look, I'm sure you can come up with a reason why you two were together that night. You could say something needed fixing or that you had car trouble. He works here, for Christ's sake."

"It's not that easy; we have a history. A history that everyone in this town knows about." She shakes her head, looking helpless.

"Are you scared of your husband?" I ask her outright, there ain't no use holding back.

"No, I'm not." She looks up at me and scowls.

"Now say that again and try and sound more convincing." I don't care that I'm being a bitch, she needs to do what's right and not just by Cole but by herself, too.

"I don't think anybody's husband would be ok with their wife being alone with a man who they were in love with."

"*Were* in love with?" I question, resting my hands on her table. "If you still got any of that love for him left, you won't let him go down for this." I leave her on that and head for the door, but before I open it, there's something else I need to ask.

"Is Leia gonna be ok?" All the Mason brothers seem to have an edge about them. I guess most would say that about the Carson brothers, too, but I don't like the way Aubrey Mason keeps her eyes to the floor like she's afraid to look up.

"She'll get used to it." The sadness in her tone makes me even more determined to get Wade to speak to her. Hell, I'll speak to her myself if I have to.

"Maybe *you* should be the one who's careful," Aubrey calls out to me before I can leave.

"Garrett would never hurt me." I look back at her with pity. I can't imagine why anyone would commit themselves to a lifetime of misery.

"Maybe not, but there are plenty of people who wanna hurt him, and you'd be a real good place to start." She looks like she has pity for me, too, and her words send a shiver down my spine. I nod my head in gratitude and hope she thinks about what I've said when I leave.

I storm across the yard towards the exit. I can't call Garrett, it's been too short a time, and he'll know I've lied, so I take out my cell and call Leia instead.

"You seem to be on the wrong ranch!" A voice calls out to me, and when I turn around and see Joe Mason walking out of the stable, I feel myself start to panic.

"I just called in on your wife to see how she was doing." I put on a smile and act casual.

"That's nice, real nice, ain't it, Seth?" When I turn and look over my shoulder, the huge guy who Garrett tied up in the woods has stepped up behind me, and all of a sudden, I feel trapped.

"Well, you know, I'm new in town and just looking to make some friends."

"Sensible thinking; the Carson Ranch could do with some of those."

"Maisie!" I feel relieved when a sharp yell comes from the stable, and I see Cole marching toward us.

"Whatcha doin' here?" he asks, dragging at my arm. I can tell from the look on his face that he's not happy about me being here.

"She came to make friends with Aubrey," Joe answers him, making my excuse for being here sound so pathetic.

"Garrett know you're here?" he checks.

"Garrett's not my keeper. I'm a free woman, as all women should be." I make sure I'm looking Joe Mason right in his eyes when I say that, and he doesn't let the phoney smile drop from his lips.

"Come on, I'll take ya home." Cole pulls me away toward one of the trucks that are in the yard.

"I'll be takin' an hour out of your wages for the trouble!" Joe calls out to him as he drags me past Seth, and the beast of a man lifts his hat to me and smiles. "Be seeing you, ma'am," he nods before he places it back on.

"What the fuck ya doin' here, Maisie?" Cole scolds me, as he pulls out the yard. "Does Garrett know you're here?"

"Garrett dropped me off," I tell him, leaving out the part that I lied to him about why and trying to be smart.

"He what?" Cole nearly swerves us off the road.

"I told him Aubrey invited me and Leia over for lunch," I admit, figuring the truth will come out eventually.

"Hell, he's gonna be mad." Cole shakes his head and sighs.

"Not if we don't tell him. I was just trying to help."

"Help how?" he snaps, and now I'm gonna have to tell another lie, but at least this one has a little truth to it,

"My best friend is marrying one of those assholes. I wanted to speak to Aubrey and check she'll be ok."

"Oh, you're the meddlin' kind, ain't ya?" He breathes out tiresomely, speeding down the open road so fast my head almost hits the roof from the bumps we go over.

"I wouldn't call it meddling. I just like to look after the people I care about."

"Well, so does Garrett, and that's *exactly* why I don't want to see ya back at the Mason Ranch again."

"Come home, Cole, you can't like working there," I tell him softly, and he ignores me.

"She's never gonna leave her husband, and you're torturing yourself by being there and watching. You have a family. Garrett and Wade love you. Just come home and let yourself heal."

"It's looking to me like Copper Ridge is finally starting to get a little of its happiness back. Trust me, you don't want me there," he tells me sadly, and the atmosphere it creates makes arguing seem pointless.

When he eventually pulls up at the gate, I turn and face him.

"Don't worry, I'll keep ya secret. Last thing you want is Garrett gettin' all grizzly on ya," he half smiles at me.

"Come for dinner tomorrow night. It'll be nice to have you all together."

"Convince Josie to make her lasagne, and you gotta deal," he half smiles as I open the door to the truck and slide out.

"You remember what I said. You stay out of it, okay? I like ya, you're good for my brother, and you're good for this place." He looks up at the gate with the Copper Ridge sign on it.

"I'll see you tomorrow," I smile, shutting the door and letting him drive away.

"This is nice." Maisie looks up at me. We're not doing anything special, just watching a movie, but she looks happy, and that's all I care about. I can't remember the last time I watched a movie, and I ain't really watching this one. It's hard to focus when I got her sitting on the floor between my legs, wearing one of my shirts and a pair of fluffy socks. I love the way her lips move when she laughs and how she keeps glancing up to see if I find it funny, too. I even love the nibbling noises she makes eating from the big bowl of popcorn she's got on her lap.

"You sure you don't want any?" She holds up the bowl, and I take it from her hands, place it beside me and drag her up to sit on my lap.

"That's better," I kiss her cheek and get back to watching the movie, smoothing my hands over her thighs, and when the door opens and Cole bursts through it, I just know that my perfect night is about to be ruined.

"Why ain't ya answerin' your phone?" he yells at me.

"It's chargin' in the kitchen. What's the problem?" Cole looks around the living room, like he's startled by what he's seeing.

"It's Wade. Noah just rang, he was in Cahoots earlier

lookin' for a fight, and when no one was bitin', he moved on to look somewhere else."

"And they let him leave?" I shift Maisie off my lap so I can stand up.

"No, they're following him. He's heading toward Columbus, but they thought we'd be better at talkin' some sense into him than they would."

"Shit." I shake my head and look at Maisie apologetically.

"You need to go find him," she tells me, "I can pause the movie."

I wanna tell her that it ain't the movie I'm pissed off about missing, but if I do that in front of my brother, I'll never hear the end of it.

"I'll go get changed." I head straight upstairs to throw on some jeans and a shirt. Maisie assured me I couldn't chill out and watch a movie properly unless I slobbed it out in my sweatpants, and I have to admit, I liked the way it felt slobbing it out with her.

I get dressed quickly, knowing how hot-headed Wade can get when he's on one, and when I come back down the stairs, I find Maisie and Cole standing in silence.

"Be careful." Maisie comes to the bottom of the stairs to kiss me goodbye while Cole heads toward the door. I kiss her again before grabbing my hat and stepping out the door.

"You know you're turnin' into a cinnamon roll, right?" Cole shakes his head at me as I jump into the passenger seat, and he gets behind the wheel.

"Fuck you." I respond, checking he's got a gun in his glove box just in case.

We arrive at the bar where The River Boys have followed Wade and step into chaos. Wade is beating the hell out of a guy on the floor, and the River Boys are throwing fists, too. There's broken barstools, smashed bottles and blood, and I make my way through the carnage to pull my brother off the guy he's attacking. Some joker comes at me with a baseball bat, and I snatch the thing outta his hand before he can hit me, then use it to smash him across his own face.

I reach down to where Wade is on his knees, laying blow after blow into the guy on the floor and, grabbing him by his scruff, I drag him off. He spins round and tries to lay one on me, but when he sees who's gotta hold of him, he retracts.

"What the fuck is all this about?" I yell at him over the noise. He don't answer my question, just stares back at me with venom.

"Come on, we're goin' home." I drag him toward the bar and hand him off to Cole, taking my wallet out of my back pocket. I slam the ranch's business card onto the bar.

"You send the bill for any damages here. Sorry 'bout the disruption," I tell the distraught-looking barmaid before seeking out Noah and nodding my head at the door, letting him know it's time for us to leave. I step outside, and when Cole follows after me, he shoves Wade out the doors, so he stumbles onto the ground.

"Get yourself together; we got enough shit to deal with without lookin' for fights!" he shouts at him.

"What the fuck would you know about the shit this family gotta deal with, Cole? You're too busy fuckin' someone else's wife," Wade spits back at him, and there ain't nothing anyone can do to stop the fist that Cole throws at his face.

"Hey, come on." I step between 'em when Wade goes to retaliate, and I'm surprised but relieved when Cole backs down.

"Wade, you're letting the family down and making a fool outta yourself right now." I keep my voice calm and try to reason with him. He shakes his head at me and laughs before ripping his shirt off and slamming his palm over the spot on his chest where he's branded.

"What *I'm* doing is taking this shit seriously!" he yells, his eyes raw with anger and all the muscles in his body tense.

"You're at home playin' happy fuckin' ever after, and bein' someone you ain't, all while that cunt that knocked up our baby sister is out there breathin'. *You* may have given up on finding him, but *I* didn't." He finishes his rant with his chest rising and falling rapidly, and I can relate to all the pain and anger he's feeling. I've never given up on getting answers. I think about Bree and the fact she ain't here anymore every day, but fighting our way through every town in fucking Montana ain't gonna get us answers, and I *know* Breanna ain't the reason he's here tonight. He needs to feel a different kinda pain to the one that's in his heart, and I can relate to that, too.

"This ain't about Breanna, and you know it. This is about Leia Walker marryin' a man that ain't you. This is about all the feelin's you got inside ya that you don't know what to do with. You can walk into a bar and throw your fists around to prove you're a man, but that don't change the fact ya ain't man enough to do anything about her." He grabs the front of my shirt and pulls back his fist like he's gonna hit me, but I don't flinch.

"Go ahead, if you think it's gonna make you feel better. But I can promise ya it won't. Only thing that's gonna make all that hurt go away, is taking what you want."

"I ain't even on her radar." Wade releases me and lowers his hand.

"Ya don't know that till ya tell her," I point out, noticing that a crowd has gathered around us, and the River Boys are watching, too.

"Come on, let's go home." I nod my head at the River Boys to thank 'em for their efforts tonight before opening the passenger door of the truck, so Wade can get inside.

"I'm sorry I whacked ya," Cole growls under his breath as we're driving home.

"I'm sorry for what I said to both of ya." Wade keeps his head low, and his shoulders bump between mine and Cole's as he sits in the middle of us. "And that schoolgirl punch didn't hurt anyway." He raises his head, and a tiny snigger lifts on his lips.

"Maybe I should hit ya with another one and shut you the fuck up," Cole scoffs a laugh, and just like that everything's right between us again. It's the way it's always been and the way it'll stay.

When we get back to the ranch, Cole agrees to spend the night and heads upstairs, while Wade takes himself to the bathroom to clean the blood off himself. He's got some cuts and bruises but nothing that needs stitches. I make my way up to bed, stopping in the door frame and smiling when I see Maisie laid out asleep on my mattress. I don't care that she's on my side. I'll make a new side. There's loads of changes I'm prepared to make for that girl. Getting undressed as quietly as I can, I slide in beside her, wrapping my arms around her and pulling her close. She stirs a little, but she doesn't wake up, and as I lie in the dark with her in my arms, feeling her breath, I feel a little guilty. My brothers deserve this too. We've all been through our fair share of shit, and I'm sure there'll be plenty more of it to come. I want them to be happy, they both know how to love, that ain't questionable. But they should know how it feels to love without hurt.

"Is everyone ok?" Maisie asks sleepily.

"It's all good, baby. Go back to sleep." I kiss the top of her head and hold her a little tighter.

"Was it over Leia?" she asks, reaching across me to turn on the lamp, then propping herself up on my chest.

"What do you think?" I tilt my head and raise my eyebrows.

"We're gonna have to fix it. I'll talk to Leia see if she..."

"You gotta let 'em figure it out for themselves, same way we did."

The last thing I want is Maisie caught up in any Mason drama. I wasn't happy about her going to Aubrey's for lunch earlier, but I've discovered that you can't clip this girl's wings, and even if I could, I wouldn't.

"You think we have it figured out?" she asks, with that soft smile on her lips.

"You're here, ain't ya. And this may be new for us, but we've wanted it for long enough to make sure it works." Maisie seems satisfied with my answer.

"So, what's troubling you?" She proves I'm shit at hiding my emotions.

"Wade brought up Breanna tonight." I let out out a heavy sigh and allow the hurt to sink in. He's right, it's been so long, and we're no closer to finding out who got my sister pregnant. What he's wrong about is me giving up. I think about finding the fucker and making him pay night and day.

"You want to talk about it?" She looks concerned, and I don't wanna burden her with this, but I hear that talkin' shit out helps, and Maisie wants no secrets between us, so I'll give it a go.

"The reason Ronnie Mason went lookin' for Bree's autopsy

report is because he caught Aubrey lookin' for it online. That strikes me as strange, don't it to you?"

"It's certainly suspicious. Were they friends? I thought Aubrey was Cole's age."

"She is, but her mom and mine were close, and Breanna grew up with three older brothers. She looked at Aubrey like a sister."

"So, do you think she knew about the baby?" Maisie's interest is piqued, I can tell. I don't think she knows it, but she's a fixer. "Because even if she did, looking for the autopsy report is still kinda weird."

"You're right, there; maybe Wade had a point earlier. I'm not tryin' hard enough to find the fucker who got her pregnant."

"Garrett, you've gotta lot to deal with around here. You're doing all you can, and even if you do find out who the father was, what are you gonna do about it?" I look at her innocent face and her big, blue eyes wishing I had a different answer for her.

"No secrets?" I check she still wants to keep that rule in place, especially when it comes to this kinda shit.

"No secrets," she confirms, with a smile.

"I'm gonna kill him." My voice comes out raspy. I will shelter and protect Maisie from anything, but I won't lie about who I am. If I'm gonna expect this girl to spend the rest of her life with me, she deserves honesty.

She doesn't say anything back, just smiles at me sadly, then kisses me to let me know that's ok.

CHAPTER 16

MAISIE

Dalton's helping me load the groceries into the truck when I notice Aubrey Mason coming out of the station across the street. She looks around warily as she heads toward her car, like she's scared someone might see her, and thinking about what Garrett said to me last night, I excuse myself from Dalton to rush across and speak with her.

"Hey!" I call out to her before she can get inside. She doesn't look the slightest bit happy to see me, but I can't let that bother me.

"I did it, okay? I spoke to Sheriff Nelson and told them where Cole was that night." Her confession takes me by surprise, and I can't hold back. I launch at her and hug her right there, on the street.

"Thank you." I pull back when I realize I'm probably making her uncomfortable and smile awkwardly.

"I love him, you know," she whispers sadly, and I see her sincerity.

"I know," I smile back at her sadly. Since I've been back in town, I've been so swept off my feet by Garrett, and his change of heart, that I've almost forgotten what it feels like to be heartbroken.

"Will this get you into trouble?" I check. The last thing I

want is for this to get her into trouble with her husband and his family.

"I don't know." She tries to look brave, and I can see how scared she is.

"You've done the right thing, and if you do find yourself in trouble, I know Cole will take care of you. Garrett would, too." I hope it brings her some assurance.

My words don't seem to comfort her, and when she gets inside the car and sits behind the wheel, I take hold of the door to stop her from closing it.

"Why were you looking for Breanna's autopsy on Mr. Mason's computer?" I blurt out the question that's been going round and round in my head since I spoke to Garrett last night. He needs answers, and if there's any way I can get them for him, I will.

"How did you...?"

"Mr. Mason found the autopsy report, and he gave it to Garrett," I inform her, causing her to look even more confused.

"How did he...? Why would he have given that to Garrett?" she asks, too perplexed to answer my original question.

"I don't know, but I need to know why you were looking for it. Just imagine losing a sister. Wouldn't you want answers, too.?"

"I did lose a sister." She closes her eyes and takes a breath, and I feel bad for forgetting how close Garrett told me they were.

"I looked for the report at Ronnie's because we don't have a computer. Joe hates technology, and I needed to know if she'd gone through with it."

"Gone through with what?" I have an idea what she means, but I need to hear it from her.

"She came to me and told me..."

"About the baby?" I intervene when I see she's finding it

hard to talk about. Aubrey nods her head and chews on the inside of her cheek.

"I know I should have told Cole, but she trusted me, and I was worried about what he might do."

"Do you know who the father was?" I feel like I could be getting somewhere here, and I wonder what the hell I'll do if I am. Sharing the information with Garrett would be sentencing a man to death. I don't know if I want that on my conscience.

"She wouldn't tell me, but I had suspicions." Aubrey looks away like she's ashamed.

"Who?" I reach for her arm and clutch it desperately. Aubrey is unpredictable; she could clam up at any time.

"Look, Maisie, you seem like a real nice girl, so I'm gonna do you a favor and warn you to stay out of this." She reaches for the handle to try and close the door, but I keep a firm hold of it.

"Tell me." My tone changes from friendly to desperate.

"She was getting an abortion because the man she was seeing was married, and he refused to leave his wife. I wanted to check the report to see if she'd gone through with it because if she hadn't, I'd question if she jumped off Blackdrop Point or if she was pushed." The stone-cold look she gives me suddenly makes everything clear.

"You think it was Joe," I speak my thoughts out loud, stepping back in shock, and she takes advantage of my shock and pulls sharply at the handle, closing the door and starting her engine. I stand in the road and watch her drive away, and it isn't until I hear a loud honk of a horn and feel hands on my shoulders that I realize I'm blocking the traffic.

"You ok? That looked kinda heated." Dalton holds his hand up in apology to the car as he helps me across the street and back to the truck.

"I'm fine." I try and shake off the feeling of fear that's just come over me. Joe Mason *can't* be the person who got Breanna pregnant. I was expecting it to be someone my age, some college kid. Not a married man. I've even suspected Dalton a few times.

"You knew Breanna, you liked her, right?" I ask him.

"Yeah, I liked her. I liked her a lot," he tells me, searching my face for an explanation.

"Did you know she was pregnant when she died?" I check. I don't know if Garrett has told anyone else about the report, and I don't care if I get in trouble for it. Garrett can't stay mad at me for long anyway, and I need to get to the bottom of this.

"I should get you back to the house." Dalton's face drops, and he quickly moves around the truck to get behind the wheel.

"Dalton, tell me." I get into the passenger seat beside him, not prepared to give up on this.

"Shut up!" he yells at me viciously, and it shocks the hell out of me.

"Shit! I'm sorry, I didn't mean to yell at ya." He looks up at me with a red face and an apologetic smile.

"I know you cared about her. I was just wondering."

"It weren't mine, if that's what you were thinking." He starts the truck and pulls out, and seeing how sad he suddenly looks, I decide to keep my mouth shut for the rest of the journey home.

Wade doesn't come home for dinner, so it's just me and Garrett, and I try to judge his mood before I start questioning him. I've had all afternoon to think about my conversation with Aubrey, and it's all that's been spinning around in my head.

"How was your day?" I ask, pushing my fork around the salad I requested Josie make me. I swear, if I eat red meat again this week, I'll start mooing.

"Good, I got a ranch hand. He's green, but he looks like he's got some work in him," Garrett assures me, reaching for his glass of wine and taking a sip.

"I hear you were speakin' to Aubrey Mason today," he mentions casually, but I can tell from his scowl that there's nothing casual about it.

"Is that a crime?" I smile at him seductively.

"No, it ain't. You two just seem to be gettin' close," he points out, clearing his throat before tucking back into his dinner.

"I don't think anyone gets close to Aubrey, well no one except Cole, anyway." I notice the tiny smirk he makes and realize that he's not completely furious.

"Dalton rat me out?" I ask, trying not too look pissed about it. Though I did think Dalton was my friend.

"Don't blame him, it's in his job description." Garrett places his knife and fork down on his plate when he's finished, then leans over it, fisting his hands together and resting his chin on them. The look he gives me across the table suggests he's waiting on an explanation.

"Ok, so I *may* have asked her why she was looking for the report...but only because I want to help you. I could see how tense you were last night, and if that's another thing that's keeping Wade back from the rodeo, I wanted to do what I could." I speak fast before he can interrupt me.

"Maisie, I don't want you involved in this," he tells me, shaking his head and looking frustrated.

"Well, I am involved." I get up from my chair and go to sit on his lap. "I love you." I decide it's time I told him, although I'm sure he already knows it. I'm hardly playing the hard-to-get game I intended.

"You know, I planned on tellin' you that first." He looks up at me and smiles.

"Well, you took too long, seems to be a habit with you." I wiggle my eyebrows at him sarcastically.

"I do, though. I love ya. All of ya. Even the annoying, persistent, meddle maker part." He tucks a strand of hair behind my ear and looks at me seriously. "Which is exactly why I gotta ask you to stay out of this," he whispers.

"Garrett, I get that you care about me, and I love it. But I'm not this helpless, innocent girl you think needs wrapping up in cotton wool. I want to help this family heal." I slide my hand into the front of his shirt and touch the bumpy scar on his chest. "I know how much all this means to you, and I wanna play my part in it."

Garrett's hand raises up and clutches mine through his shirt.

"My job's to protect you. Please just trust me on this. Stay out of it." His eyebrows furrow the way they always do when he's worried.

"Besides, you did enough when you got Aubrey to speak to the Sheriff." He raises his eyebrows at me, and I figure it's pointless me denying it.

"How did you find that out?" I sigh.

"Sheriff called about an hour ago, said Aubrey went in and said Cole was with her that night. I thought it was coincidental, since you only had lunch with her yesterday."

"Jesus, is there anyone in this town who doesn't leap to your command?" I roll my eyes and go to get up, but Garrett holds me firm. He pushes his plate to one side and then reaches over the table for mine, dragging it in front of me and picking up my fork.

"Finish ya food," he orders, picking up my fork and holding it out to me, and when I snatch it out his hand before stabbing it into my salad, I answer my own question.

I wait until Maisie's in a deep sleep before I get out of bed, slip into some clothes and head downstairs.

"It's late. Where ya headed?" Wade asks from the couch when I pass him on my way to the door.

"Got a message from Noah earlier this evening. Zayne managed to do his thing and hack Swann's files." I keep my voice down as I pull on my jacket and put my hat on.

"Ya want me to come with?" He's already on his feet, but I shake my head.

"No, I want ya to stay here and keep an eye on Maisie. I don't like leavin' her alone."

"Ya worried someone wants to hurt her?" Wade looks concerned himself, him and Maisie have always been close.

"I don't know, but someone killed Cora." I shrug, letting him know I ain't about to take any risks.

"C'mon Garrett, there's plenty of people who wanted Cora dead. She's been pissin' people off since she came into town. If ya didn't have money and power, she treated ya like shit, and if ya did, the woman was ruthless. She tried it on with you enough times for ya to know that."

"Will you shut your mouth?" I whisper yell at him, checking the landing to make sure Maisie ain't listening.

"Why does it matter if Maisie knows or not? Ain't like ya acted on it. Ya put that whore right in her place."

"It matters because that's her mother and believe me when I say no one hated her more than I did, but she deserves to have some good memories." I loosen up a little when he nods his head like he understands.

I drive out to the lake house where Noah lives, and I ain't surprised when I hear the thumping music and see he's got a houseful of people. The River Boys know how to party; they're young and out for a good time, and I can't blame 'em for that. Although Noah is always present, he ain't like the other two. His place may be the hangout, but he's always detached from the fun. I don't know where he came from or how he ended up doing the mayor's dirty work, but what I do know is he's one hell of an asset.

"Evenin'" I tip my chin at him when I find him standing out on his porch all alone.

"Sup?" He blows out a thick cloud of smoke and offers out the blunt he's been dragging on.

"Ain't done that shit in years." I shake my head in refusal.

"Maybe ya should, might mellow ya out a little." The cocky shit sniggers at me before getting down to what I came here for.

"Here." I take the USB stick that he hands me. "He managed to get all the files from the case," he assures me.

"How much?" I ask, knowing this would have taken some time and maybe even an outside source. Zayne's good when it comes to this kinda shit, but hacking investigators is another level.

"You don't owe anythin'." Noah creases his forehead and taps his chest over the tight black tee he's wearing.

I nod my appreciation. When I offered the River Boys the brand in exchange for my help, I questioned whether or not it was the right thing to do. They keep on proving to me I was right to trust my instinct.

"You take a look for yourself?" I ask, sliding the USB into my pocket.

"Had to check I wasn't a suspect myself; the bitch sure questioned me like I was when she came here," Noah responds.

"And?"

"We're all clear," he assures me, "your brother's still marked, but I assume Aubrey's visit to Nelson has put him in the clear."

"How d'ya hear about that?"

"Ya think you're the only one who's got Nelson in his pocket? He's a wise man," Noah smiles cleverly before taking another toke on his spliff.

"So, who are the suspects?" I know I have the resources to find out for myself now, but I'm impatient.

"Oh, you'll like this one... Jason fuckin' McIntyre," Noah huffs a laugh.

"And unless he dug himself up, we both know it ain't him." He leans forward to rest his arms on his porch rail and looks out onto the lake. "You'll find out for yourself when you go through the files, but I may as well tell you now. The reason he's a suspect is because there was a large transfer of money made from Cora to him a few years back, and her phone records show that just recently she was trying to get back in touch with him."

"Cora and Jason? That makes no sense."

"She paid him five grand a week before your pops had his office ransacked." I spin my head when I figure out what he's telling me, and the worse thing about it is that it doesn't surprise me.

"Sneaky fuckin' bitch!" I shake my head and try to cull the rage building up inside me. I gotta go home to Maisie, and I can't take it with me.

"Since the police can't find him, and your brother is clear, I guess they're a little stuck." Noah flicks his finished blunt into one of the bushes and turns to face me.

"You know Cora was spending a whole lotta time with old man Mason before she died?" he informs me.

"I'm starting to wonder if you're as bad as Dolores." I snigger.

"Nah, Mayor Walker has me keepin' an eye on the old man from time to time. I don't think he trusts him as much as we all think. Either that or he was jealous."

Everyone in Fork River suspects that Cora and Walker were at it, and although he's never done anything to hide his affection for her, no one would ever accuse him of it. He has a squeaky-clean reputation that he works very hard to maintain. Hidden behind all the politics, fancy suits, and the perfect family is a man who, deep down, ain't no better than us. Walker turns a blind eye to things me and my family do, and I know it's because he figures one day, he might need us.

Noah doesn't have to share this information with me, and the fact he does makes me trust him even more. Some may call him a loose cannon, but all I've ever got out of him is loyalty.

"Is he a suspect, too?"

"Who, Walker?" Noah laughs and shakes his head. "You know that man don't get his hands dirty, and he has a firm alibi. He was the auctioneer at some charity ball Kristen's college hosted."

"I wasn't, for a second, thinkin' he'd done it himself." I give Noah a suspicious look.

"I can tell ya that on this occasion, my hands ain't dirty either. Swann's lookin' into some of her ex-husbands, though. Turns out Cora left a couple of 'em in financial trouble," he adds.

"Well, I don't care who killed her, just so long as Swann

don't think it's any of us, and whoever it was, ain't gonna come after Maisie."

"I think you're clear on that, Cora had a lot of enemies, but I see no reason why they'd wanna hurt ya girl." Pushing himself off the rail to stand up straight. "You wanna stick around for a beer?" he offers.

"Nah, I gotta shoot, appreciate this, though." I leave him to get back to his party and head back to my truck.

When I get back home, I'm surprised to find Maisie awake, sitting on the couch and watching TV. She picks up the remote and points it at the screen to turn it off before rushing toward me. Leaping onto my body, she wraps her arms around my neck and her legs around my hips.

"Where did you sneak off to?" She asks so sweetly that I wanna devour her. Right here, right now, on my living room floor.

"Where's Wade?" I take a look around for any sign of him as I carry her over to the drinks counter and rest her ass on its surface.

"He went to bed not long after I woke up." She takes the hat off my head and tosses it on the couch before I slide the oversized tee she's wearing higher up her thighs and kiss her lips.

"You miss me?" I pull away to ask, and when she shakes her head, I squeeze her hips so hard that she squeals.

"Okay, maybe I missed you a little," she admits, and as a reward for her honestly, I let my hand slip between her legs. When I discover she's not wearing any panties, I raise my eyebrows at her, and teasingly slip my finger between the thin strip of hair she's got on her pussy lips.

"Feels like you missed me more than just a little bit," I point out when she soaks my finger.

She shrugs, and the cute smile on her face makes my heart

ache. All this feels too good to be real. I'm just waiting for it to be snatched away, and I don't know how to fix that. Still, it seems a small sacrifice when I compare it to the pain of not having her.

"I need to go to the doctor" she blurts out, taking me by surprise and instantly making me worry.

"Are ya sick?" I step back so I can check her over.

"No, but if we keep doing this, somethings probably gonna happen, and I should get one of those shots that prevent it. I know you said you'd sort it but..." I slam my mouth over hers to stop her from talking. She's right, I made her promise a few days ago that I'd take care of birth control, and I haven't. Truth of the matter is, I don't like the thought of preventing it from happening. I've had a vision for three years of how I wanted my life to look, and I've wasted too much time already.

I take her mind off doctors and shots by stroking her clit, and when she starts to fumble with my belt to free me, I know I've been successful. I help her take out my cock, stroking it through my palm as I near her entrance, and when she tightens the grip her legs have around my hips, I push inside her.

I take her much harder than I have before. Her body's starting to get used to me now, I don't have to be so easy on her, and judging from the noises she's making, I'm assuming she likes it.

"Shhh! You'll wake Wade." I slam my hand over her mouth, pressing my forehead tight to hers as I thrust deep inside her. My other arm wraps around her hips, pushing her tighter against me to ensure she gets every inch.

I fuck her fast and hard, and when she comes, she sinks her teeth into my palm and stares fiercely into my eyes. I can feel my own release coming, and I know I should pull out. Maisie doesn't think she's ready yet, I shouldn't go against her wishes, but the thought of knocking her up has me thrusting my hips even deeper.

"There's no limits." I don't realize I've said my thoughts out loud until I see the confusion on her face, and when I feel my cock spasm, pulsing hot cum deep into her unprotected pussy, I know that no matter how hard I try, I'll never truly be a good man.

"No limits to what?" she asks when I drop my head onto her shoulder and try to catch my breath.

"No limits to what I'd do to keep you." I manage, lifting my head back up to see her reaction. I don't know if she understands what that means for her or not, but she doesn't protest when I hold her legs tightly anchored around my hips, so my cock remains rooted as deep inside her as I can get it.

CHAPTER 18

MAISIE

"Please, I love the fair," I beg Garrett as we ride back into the yard. I insisted on riding out with him this morning, and if I'm gonna make this my permanent home, I'm gonna have to know a little about how the place gets run. I also need to have a conversation with Garrett about the birth control situation. We're playing a risky game, but I can sense he's not in the best of moods today. So instead of bringing it up, I try cheering him up. Everyone loves the fair, right?

"So do all the bunkhouse boys. I give 'em the time off every year, which means this place needs me here."

"Hey, you guys goin' to the fair tonight?" Dalton looks up from the horse that he's grooming to ask us, and I don't miss the way Garrett rolls his eyes as he jumps off Thunder.

"Thanks for that," he snarls at Dalton before handing him his reins and reaching up his arms to lift me down from Darcy. I make sure my body brushes tight against his as I slide down it.

"We can't go, Garrett's busy," I do a little eye-rolling of my own before leading Darcy into the stable.

It's getting dark outside, and I've spent the whole afternoon organizing the ranch's admin into a system I can work with. I called Savannah and told her I wouldn't be coming back to L.A. I didn't want to leave her struggling, so I offered to pay her

106

a few more months' rent while she looks for someone to take my room, but she assures me she's got it covered.

She's probably enjoying all that time she's getting alone with her boyfriend without me moping around the place.

"You ready?" I look up when I see Garrett standing in the door, he looks so handsome in the black shirt and jeans he's got on, and he's wearing his black hat, too.

"Ready for what?" I haven't seen him all day. I figured he was best left alone as he's clearly got something on his mind.

"For the fair, it's where you wanna go, ain't it?" I feel the smile tug on my lips, but I don't race over to hug him like I want to.

"I thought you were too busy?" I shrug like it doesn't bother me either way.

"Wade offered to take care of things, and since you got all pouty with me out in the yard, I figured I'd better take him up on it."

"I was not pouty." When I cross my arms over my chest and huff, he laughs at me.

"Come on darlin', the fair only comes once a year." He gestures his head toward the front door, and I give up pretending I'm not desperate to go, quickly closing the laptop and grabbing my phone before he changes his mind.

The Grand Fair of Fork River isn't a fraction of the size of the ones we have in L.A., but there's plenty to do, and I think even Garrett is enjoying himself a little. He laughs at me when I try to stay on the bucking bronco, then builds up quite the crowd when he takes the saddle himself and shows that he wasn't kidding when he said he used to be good at it. Then eventually, after me asking him all night, he agrees to take me on the Ferris Wheel.

"This would be a good time to tell a girl you love her," I tell him, feeling on top of the world when we reach the top and have all the bright lights below us.

"Do I need to tell ya?" He kisses me and proves that actions speak louder than words.

"Still, it doesn't hurt to say it. I don't think I could ever tire of hearing you say those words to me."

"I love you," he tells me, with a dead-serious look in his eyes.

"Why do I get the impression those words scare you?" I ask.

"Because they do. They petrify me," he admits, and the arm he's got wrapped around my shoulder grips a little tighter.

"Is that why your palms are sweating?" I giggle, releasing the hand I've got placed over my shoulder so I can hold his and wiping it on his jeans.

"No, they're sweatin' because I *hate* fuckin' heights!" he confesses, and when I crack up, laughing, it makes the cart swing, and Garrett grabs the safety bar. Sure, he's been putting off getting on here since we arrived, but he showed no fear when we got on.

"Then what the hell are you doing two hundred feet in the air, riding a Ferris Wheel?" I ask him, still smiling.

"Because the girl I love wanted to." He touches that cold, sweaty palm to my cheek and kisses me. "And I'm all about conquering my fears these days." The look he gives me makes the warm feeling in my chest spread out to the rest of my body, and I tuck myself into his chest and enjoy the rest of the ride.

I'm carrying the huge bear he won for me on the shooting range when we bump into Leia and Caleb. He walks with arrogance, looking down his nose at people like he's better than them, and although he's only a few years older than me, he looks so out of place here among, all this fun. "Hey," Leia looks excited to see me, and when she pulls me in for a hug, she almost sucks all the breath out of my lungs.

"You guys wanna hang out?" She sounds so hopeful, and I'm about to say yes when Garrett interrupts me.

"Actually, we were just about to head home. I can't leave Wade to do everything by himself tonight."

"I'm surprised he ain't here. Wade loves the fair. We usually come together." Leia looks a little sad, and Caleb has a smug look on his face that I really hate the look of.

"Yeah, well, Wade don't mind makin' a sacrifice once in a while," Garrett answers in a hostile tone as he stares Caleb Mason square in the eye. I grab his hand and squeeze it tight, hoping he'll remember that this is my friend's fiancé.

"You guys have a great night, though," I tell Leia, hoping this awkward thing the Carsons have with the Masons isn't gonna ruin our friendship.

It takes us a while to leave, Garrett seems to know everyone in town, and they all want to speak to him.

"Well, shoot me on the spot. What's this, I see? Garrett Carson courtin'?" An old woman with gray hair and glasses smiles at him warmly as we pass through the gates heading back to the truck.

"Maisie, this is Dolores," he introduces us, throwing me a look that tells me to humor her.

"I remember you used to come by the diner when you were in town a few summers ago," she tells me.

"I did. I didn't think you'd remember me," I laugh.

"Dolores don't forget a thing," Garrett raises his eyebrows, and it earns him a hard nudge from the old woman's elbow.

"Well, it's good to see someone putting a smile on his face." She nods her head to me as we move on and when we get to the truck, I toss the bear into the back and grab Garrett by the hand. He's taken off guard when I drag him into the shadows behind the tailgate of the truck, kissing him while I start to undo his belt.

"Whatcha doin?" he asks, checking around us in case anyone's about.

"You ever gotten head at the fair before?" I look up at him as I lower onto my knees in front of him and think about what he did to me in the mayor's bathroom.

"No. You ever given it?" The questionable look on his face tells me he doesn't like the idea of that, and I take pleasure in that jealous possessiveness he has. I shake my head before I take his cock in my hand and start to work it through my fist. He's already hard, but it grows even more in size as I pump him slowly and edge him toward my lips.

"*Jesus fucking Christ!*" he curses, scrunching my hair in his fist as I take as much of him as I can manage, pulling back slowly and sucking him hard. I have no idea if what I'm doing is right, I've never had a man's cock in my mouth before, but when Garrett starts to moan the same way he does when he's inside my pussy, I figure I'm doing something right.

I try so hard to take all of him, but he's too big, and I end up gagging. Garrett seems to really like that, too, because he takes my head in both his hands and takes control, making sure I gag, again and again.

"You're a fuckin' bad girl, Maisie Wildman." He grabs at my arms and pulls me up from the ground, then stepping his body around mine so he's behind me, he takes my hands and places them on the top of the tailgate.

"You hold on tight to that," he whispers, sliding his hands down my body and popping the button on my jeans. He forces them down to my knees, and a thrill throbs inside me when I know what's coming.

"This is gonna be fast and hard because there ain't no way I can wait until we get back home," he speaks into my ear from behind me.

"But, I promise when I get you into bed, I'm gonna return that favor." I grip hard at the tailgate as he fills me with one slow, agonizing push. Then after holding himself inside me for a few seconds and feeling the way I pulse around him, he starts to pump his hips. He thrusts into me so hard and fast that I forget we're in a field full of cars when I come, and actually scream.

"Sorry," I whisper, catching my breath and biting my lip as he starts to edge me toward another orgasm.

"Scream as loud as you want darlin', I want the whole, damn town to know ya mine," he growls into my ear before he bites it, and after I've come for a second time, he reaches his arm up my body and grips his hand around my throat as he comes himself. He doesn't seem to care that I'm unprotected. I get the impression he kinda likes it, and when he spins me around and takes my face in both his hands, kissing me so hard that I go dizzy, I realize that I don't care, either.

———

When we get back to the ranch, Garrett's in a great mood; he even sang a little to the music he had playing in the truck, banging the wheel to the beat and making me laugh.

Garrett opens the front door for me and hangs up his hat before kissing me and lifting me up onto his body. He starts to carry me up the stairs, and I press kisses into his neck as he takes each step. When he suddenly comes to an abrupt halt, I lift my head to see what's troubling him.

"That's odd." He places me back on my feet and heads toward the door on the other side of the landing.

"What?"

"Breanna's bedroom door is open." I see rage on his face

111

when he looks inside, and when I step beside him and see the mess that's been made, a chill passes over my skin.

"What the hell?" He steps over the drawers that have been pulled out and into the middle of it, and I quickly rush to check the other rooms. Mine is just how I left it, and the room I share with Garrett now seems untouched, too, but when I open the door and see the mess of Bill and Mom's old room, I gasp.

"This was your mom's room," Garrett steps in behind me as we look around all the clothes and shoe boxes that are scattered around the floor, along with the broken furniture. Suddenly I feel bad for not even thinking about asking where her stuff was and wanting to go through it.

But I haven't got time to dwell on that because the distant look on Garrett's face and the way the veins in his neck are pulsing tells me all my efforts need to go into keeping him calm.

"It's ok, we can clear this up, and we'll check the rest of the house to see what's been taken."

"I ain't worried about whatever this person took. I'm worried about the fact they were here. In your home."

"*Our* home," I remind him, stepping closer to wrap my arm around his and hold his hand. I can feel his pulse beating, and his nostrils are flaring like a bull about to charge.

"What if you'd been here, like you were the night Pops..." I watch him swallow thickly as he recalls the memory.

"I wasn't, though. I was with you, safe." I clutch him a little tighter, trying hard to hide the fact that I'm freaked out by the idea of that, too. And knowing that someone has been here is making me feel uneasy.

"Why. Why were they here?" he asks me with narrow eyes that glisten with danger.

"I don't know, but it looks to me like they were lookin' for somethin'." I head out into the hall and have a quick check through the other rooms, none of them seem to have been disturbed, and when I return to Mom's old room where I left him, I find him sitting on the bed, breathing heavily. I've only seen him look this mad a few times before, and the last time he ended up killing.

"How was the fair?" I hear Wade's voice call out through the house and lean over the banister.

"You better get up here," I tell him, watching him race up the stairs when he notices the serious look on my face.

"What the fuck?" He looks as shocked as Garrett when he sees the state of my mom's old room.

"Breanna's room's the same. You didn't see or hear anything?" Garrett checks.

"No, I've been in the bunkhouse playin' hold 'em with Mitch and Otis. Did they take anything?" he asks.

"How am I supposed to know if all this crap belonged to Cora?" Garrett storms out the room, and I follow him as he heads downstairs straight for the drinking cabinet.

He pours himself a drink and downs it in one.

"Fuckin' bitch!" He throws his glass at the wall, making me jump.

"Hey, calm down. Why are you mad at her? This isn't her fault. She's dead." I go to him to try and comfort him, but he remains stiff.

"You could've been here," he repeats, growling through his teeth like it's all that matters.

"But I wasn't. It's gonna be okay."

"No, it ain't. What if whoever did this comes back, and I ain't here? Whoever this is, is clearly looking for answers, and I know how dangerous that can make a man." He shakes his head at me. "Maisie, you have no idea what kinda person your mother was. She was vicious, and she was relentless. She paid Jason McIntyre to break in here the night my pops died, and she barely waited until he was cold before she tried gettin' herself into my bed."

I suddenly stand back and put some space between us because I can't believe what I'm hearing.

"And did you?" The question trembles from my lips.

"No." Garrett looks irritated as he shakes his head.

"I'm just sayin' she would stop at nothin' to get what she wants."

"Did you kill her?" I ask him again. I know he said he didn't, and yeah, he has an alibi, but Garrett promised me no secrets, and what he's just revealed are some pretty, heavy, fucking secrets and a good reason why he'd want her dead.

"What do you fuckin' take me for? I may not be a fuckin' saint, but I got some morals."

"Maybe *you* wouldn't, but what about *them*?" I feel the tears build in my eyes.

"Who?"

"The men who wear your brand. I've heard about them. I heard how your daddy stopped it, and then you brought it back. How far would those men go for you?"

Garrett shocks me when he closes the space between us, glaring down his nose at me.

"As far I asked 'em to," he tells, me with an edge of darkness in his tone.

"But that ain't the question you should be askin' here. Yes, I hated your mom with every part of my rotten soul. I thought about killing her every damn day, and that was *before* I found out she was the one who set up the home invasion that killed my father. And shall I tell you why I never acted on those thoughts?" He grips my arm like he's scared I'll run away from him, but he should know better. I love him, even with that rotten soul.

I shake my head slowly and try to hold in my tears while I wait for his answer.

"Because I knew that if I did, I'd never have been able to look you in the eyes again. And I'd rather have slept with the devil on my doorstep than give up the hope of ever having you."

He releases me and marches out the door to the yard, slamming it so hard after him that the rafters shake.

I head out the door needing to unleash. I have to find a better way of containing my anger. I shouldn't have raised my voice to her; none of this is her fault. This all falls on Cora and whoever she pissed off enough to want her dead.

"Garrett!" Mitch calls across the yard at me, and he can probably tell by the way I'm pacing that I'm pissed off. He flicks his smoke at the ground before he starts walking towards me, and I try to calm myself enough to explain what's happened.

"Someone's been at the house." I ball my fists and remind myself to breathe.

"What do you mean? Me, Wade and Otis have been here all night," Mitch shakes his head like he thinks I'm making it up.

"I mean, someone was in my fucking house!" I snap at him, too, and when I take out my cigarettes, my hands shake from all the damage they want to do.

"They trashed Bree's room, Pops', too. They were looking for something." I manage to get a spark out of my Zippo and take a sharp drag, hoping that the smoke filling my lungs is gonna take the edge off. I can't go back inside, not while I'm this fucking mad.

"They take anything?" He scrubs his hand through his

beard, the way he always does when he's thinking something over, and I hope he's thinking with some fucking logic. Cause I sure fucking ain't!

"What if she'd have been here alone?" I ignore his question and focus on what matters, fighting hard to tamp down the fury inside me.

"Unlikely, you've barely left that girl's side since she's been back in town," Mitch smirks, and I throw my fist at the barn door in frustration.

"But there will be times," I point out, knowing that I can't always be around to protect her. "It's been quiet lately, but what about when it's not?" I sit down on one of the crates, press the back of my head against the wood cladding and look up at the stars.

"You can't keep her under 24-hour surveillance." Mitch sounds a lot more serious as he takes a seat beside me. "She's too strong-willed for it even if ya could."

He's got a point there, I feel like I've been suffocating her enough since she came back, but he doesn't understand what these three years without her have been like. No one does because I've kept it to myself.

"I regretted letting her go the second she left, and I never thought she'd give me a second chance. I don't know how to..." I struggle to get the words out because they sound so pathetic.

"Some men weren't put on this earth to love, Garrett. They just haven't got it in 'em. I've met plenty of those men, and you ain't one of 'em."

"And I guess you think you are, right?" I manage a snigger despite the fact my heart is pumping venom.

"Well, I'm fifty-one years old, and I've lived in that bunkhouse since I was fifteen. Ain't no woman I've met yet, to take me out of it." The clever look on his face suggests he's proud of that fact. "You ain't had much to look up to in regard to healthy relationships, I'll give ya that. But that don't mean you ain't got a shot at this."

"I just wanna lock her away from all the world and keep her safe." I try to explain the way it feels, giving up on worrying about how weak it makes me sound. "Bad shit tends to happen to the people I care about, and I can't take risks with her. I'm selfish for bringin' her into all this, but I can't let her go."

"Stop hatin' on yaself. Life's for livin', son, and from the looks of it, you got that second chance. Don't waste a second of it fearin' what ain't happened yet."

Mitch has always had a way of making me get my head on straight.

"The person who was here tonight only went through those two rooms. It makes no sense. There is no connection between Cora and Breanna; they never even met. Bree died more than a year before Pops re-married." I speak my thoughts out loud. If I can try to make sense of all this, I might get closer to finding out who's responsible.

"Maybe they were gonna go through every room and got disturbed?" Mitch shrugs.

"Nah, it's too coincidental, they would've had to pass mine and Cole's old rooms to get between them. And as much as I don't wanna think it, I have to take into consideration the fact that the person who killed Cora may want to hurt Maisie, too." I hate even saying the words, and I hate that I have no idea who's behind all this or their motive. But most of all, I hate that I've had my head too high in the clouds to see this coming.

"Cora got what was comin', but I don't believe for a second that whoever turned her lights out would wanna hurt your girl." Mitch shakes his head, slapping my leg as he stands up to head back toward the bunkhouse.

"Was it you?" I ask, knowing there ain't nothing Mitch wouldn't do for the sake of this ranch. He saw the poison in that woman, and he saw that she was the only hurdle we had. She was constantly looking for any illegal activity she could use to bring us down.

"I was in the bunkhouse all night, you know that." He turns around, taking off his hat, pushing back his floppy, silver hair before he replaces it.

"Only because that's what everyone else in there is saying. You're telling me none of you've ever lied for each other before?" I raise my eyebrows, hoping for an honest answer.

"Plenty, but never to you, boss." He nods his head at me and smiles before being on his way.

I stay outside a little longer, letting the cool evening air bring down the heat of my mood. Mitch is right about a lot of things but having someone here tonight has unnerved me. I need to get to the bottom of who did this, and I have to put something in place to keep Maisie safe when I can't be here. The past few months, Mitch has been singing Otis's praises, hinting for him to be brought in a little deeper. Perhaps this is an opportunity for him to prove himself. I'll speak to him tomorrow and see if he wants to take on a few extra responsibilities.

Eventually, I head back inside and find Maisie in Breanna's room. She doesn't notice me straight away; she's too busy picking up stuff off the floor.

"Come here." I make her jump when I speak, proving that despite her being so calm, she's a little freaked out by what happened here tonight.

She doesn't come to me, just stands and stares, holding the bear that Breanna always carried around with her when she was younger. Even when she was sixteen, she couldn't part with the tatty old thing and still kept it on her pillow.

"I'm sorry," I say the words quietly, and with feeling because Carson men don't make a habit of apologizing, then stepping toward her, I take the bear out of her hand. When I look down at it and remember the way my sister cared for it, I feel a quiver in the back of my throat. Breanna cared for everyone. When Mama left; she was stronger than any of us. She was the only thing that kept us decent. Me and my brothers may have had our disagreements, but the one thing we all agreed on was protecting her. It brought us closer together at a time when we needed each other more than ever, and the saddest thing about it all is that we failed her.

"She loved this thing." I make a sad laugh as I place it back on the bed where it belongs, and then I scan my eyes over the pinboard that's hung above her dresser. It's full of photographs, mostly of her making groovy faces with Leia's younger sister, Karina, and a few of their other friends. There's a picture of all four of us that was taken on Pops' birthday, about a week before she died. Looking at it now, and knowing that she was pregnant when it was taken, puts a bitter taste in my mouth. And when I look at the one of her and Darcy and see Dalton in the background, the look on his face puts an uneasy thought in my head.

"You're forgiven." Maisie steps up behind me and kisses the top of my arm before admiring the photographs with me. I don't think she's ever seen Breanna before. Pops took all the pictures around the house down, and as curious as Maisie can be, I don't think she's ever been in here until tonight.

"Leia's told me a few things about her. Do you think she would have liked me?" she asks softly, sliding her finger over the picture of Breanna on Wade's back. He was, without doubt, her favorite brother; maybe it was because they were closest in age or because he was always looking for a good time.

"I think she would have loved you." I feel a lump wedge in my throat when I think of the fact they'll never meet, but I have to focus on what's important. I need to find this link. I don't know what tonight's intruder was looking for, but they were expecting to find it either here or in Cora's room.

"Did ya see Dalton tonight?" I ask, trying not to sound suspicious. I know how much Maisie likes him. I like him, too. I trust him, it's why he wears the brand, but seeing him in that photo reminds me of the way he used to look at Breanna. They were always hanging around together, and I figure it was because they were friends but what if they were more?

"At the fair?" Maisie asks, looking confused. "All the bunkhouse boys were there."

"Yeah, but did you see Dalton?"

"I... I don't know. Garrett... Are you...?"

"He liked her," I talk over her, recalling the way Wade used to tease him for it. "I need to speak to him." When I move toward the door, Maisie tugs me back.

"Not tonight, you're too angry, and I need you here with me." The worry in her eyes keeps me right where I am, and I grab her in my arms and pull her close.

"Ya got me," I promise, kissing the top of her head and breathing in the scent of her hair.

"Come on, let's get to bed. It's been a long night." I lead her out of my sister's room, then taking one last look around it, I turn off the light and close the door.

The sun hasn't even risen when I drag my ass out of bed and leave Maisie sleeping. What I need to ask Dalton has been on my mind all night. I know he'll already be up; he's always the first one out of the bunkhouse and the last one back in. He works just as hard as his uncle.

"Mornin', boss." He tips his head to me as I step into the stable.

"You go to the fair last night?" I get straight to the point, trying my best to keep my voice casual.

"No, sir." He focuses on the hay he's raking.

"Where were you?" I lean against the stable door and study him hard. Dalton doesn't strike me as someone who can tell a good lie.

"You'll only laugh at me," he sighs before shifting past me to get the wheelbarrow.

"Try me." I'm finding it progressively harder not to throttle the answer out of him.

"I've been talkin' to this girl on one of them apps, and I met up with her last night, but I don't think I'm gonna see her again." If that is the truth, he looks disappointed by it.

"I'm gonna ask ya a question, and I don't want a bullshit answer," I warn him, and when he stares back at me and nods, I pray for his sake he doesn't give me the one I've been suspecting.

"Did you have feelings for my sister?" I scrunch my forehead and bore my eyes into his, daring him to lie.

"Yes." It shocks me that he has no shame or fear when he answers.

"And did ya act on it?" I can feel my blood starting to pump a little faster.

"Thought about it plenty but never did, sir. Your father made sure of that." He looks disappointed about that, too.

"Pops?" I'm taken aback by his answer, my father was many things, but he wasn't the overprotective kind. He never gave Breanna curfews like I used to tell him he should. And I sure as hell can't imagine him warning anyone off her, not even Dalton.

"I took your sister to a party about a year before she died. It was her idea, not mine. Karina couldn't go 'cause she got grounded, and she didn't want to go alone so she..."

"Get to the fuckin' point, Dalton," I interrupt his rambling.

"Ok. So, when we got back, your father was waitin' on the porch, and I didn't realize how mad he was until he sent Bree up to bed and told me to come in here. When I did..." Dalton's eyes drop like he's ashamed to tell me what happened.

"Speak up." I feel myself losing tolerance.

"He ordered me to stand with my front against that beam, and he beat me till I bled with the training whip."

"*He what?*" I can't hide the fact I'm stunned. What he's claiming happened sounds nothing like the behavior of my father. The man didn't have a violent bone in his body.

"It's true, sir. I have no reason to lie to ya. You have my word. I won't pretend I didn't have feelings for your sister. I did, I loved her, but I can swear to ya that I never acted on it. Your pops made it clear there would be consequences if I did." The sad look on his face has me feeling a little sorry for him.

"Did you know she was pregnant?" I ask, resting my arm on the top of the stall and awaiting his answer.

"I had a hunch somethin' was wrong, we used to talk a lot, but those last few months, she shut me out." I can see how hurt he is, and it makes me forget to be mad at him for liking my sister. Truth is, she could have done a lot worse than a man like him.

"Someone broke into the house, trashed her room. I thought..." I'm ashamed to even finish the sentence. Dalton wears the brand, so I should never have doubted him.

"You thought I was the one that got her into trouble." He does me the courtesy of finishing it for me.

"I just want answers, Dalt." I shake my head and try not to show how much this is all getting to me.

"Secrets always come out in the end. You'll find out sometime, and you're just gonna have to figure out what you'll do about it when that time comes."

"And she never mentioned no boys to ya? You know, when you talked together?"

"Garrett, if I had any idea who it was, I'd find 'em and kill 'em myself." He takes the rake in his hand again and gets back to work, and I know from the look on his face that he means every word he just said.

I sit at the kitchen table and stare at the envelope with Cole's name on it. Joe didn't come home last night, so I took the time to try and put everything I need to say into words.

It's pointless trying to talk to Cole. He doesn't understand how complicated everything is. If it was simple and I could be with him, I would be. I've never stopped loving him, and I realize now that's why us starting everything up again was a mistake. It's only a matter of time before word gets out now that I've told the truth about who I was with the night Cora died. And the lame excuse I used as to why me and Cole were together may have been believed by Inspector Swann, but it won't be believed by this family. Way I see it, I've only got one option, it's the one I should have taken all those years ago. Maybe if I had, I wouldn't have put me, or Cole, through the pain we're suffering now.

I haven't worn the jeans that I find at the back of my closet since I came here, and as I slide them over my hips, I realize how much weight I've lost over the years. I flick through the hangers of dresses and blouses that I've never liked yet worn on a daily basis, until I find one of the sweaters that I used to wear before I got married. One that I couldn't part with because I knew it was Cole's favorite.

I have no idea when Joe will be home, but since the sun has

already risen, I'm assuming he'll get straight to work when he does. That's why I need to move fast. I don't want to see him before I leave.

I get on my knees and pull back the carpet from the corner of the closet, lifting the loose floorboard and reaching inside for the wooden box I keep stored here. Cole made it for me when we were younger, and although it's not exactly perfect craftsmanship, it's got my name carved in the front, and I smile whenever I look at it. Sliding my fingers over the smooth wood, I remember the day he gave it to me and how it felt to be happy.

I have some cash stashed here, nothing much, but enough to get me far away from town and keep me living for a few weeks while I look for a job. It's taken years to build it up, especially since I haven't had any money of my own. Joe didn't want me to have a job, apparently, it's not his family's way. Instead, I received an allowance for housekeeping, and I've saved what I can from it at every opportunity I could.

Taking the rolled-up dollar bills and shoving them in the bag I'll be taking with me, I pick out the photograph of me and Cole that I keep in there, too.

It's a selfie of him kissing my cheek, and the smile on my face is real.

Memories can hurt like hell; I've figured that out over the years we've been apart. I thought doing what we've been doing these past eighteen months would help, but it hasn't. It's only made me realize how badly I fucked up.

I feel bad for never explaining myself to Cole, and the fact he's never pushed me to tell him only proves how much he really loves me. I doubt he'll feel that way about me after he's read my letter. I can only hope that the pain of the truth will make me leaving him hurt a little less. My chest aches from the guilt it carries when I close my eyes and think about the night that changed everything. The same night I realized that life wasn't perfect and that I wasn't perfect, either.

"Come on, let's have another." Zoe tops up my glass with the margaritas she's made in her mom's blender. Her parents are out of town, and we're taking full advantage of a free house. I take a sip and giggle when she realizes there's no more left in the blender for herself.

"Guess I'll have to make some more," she shrugs, getting up off the floor where we're sitting and heading toward the kitchen island. I follow her through, sitting on a stool and pulling out my phone when it vibrates in my pocket. It's a message from Cole, telling me he's missing me.

"Get off that phone." Zoe snatches it out of my hands and rolls her eyes when she reads the text.

"Can you two not leave each other alone for a second?"

"One day, when you know what it feels like to be in love, I'll remind you of that," I grab my phone back, and type out a quick reply before sliding it back into my pocket.

"I am in love. With Garrett Carson. He just doesn't know it yet," Zoe sighs dreamily, and I shake my head and laugh.

"You don't stand a chance. Garrett Carson doesn't have time for girls, and even if he did, he's far too serious for someone like you."

"I disagree. Opposites attract," she winks before pressing the button on the blender and mixing us another batch.

"You really think you and him are forever?" Zoe asks thoughtfully as she tops up both our glasses.

"Of course, I do. We got it all mapped out." I move back into the living room, resting my head back on the couch.

"What about when you go to college? You know he won't be

leaving that ranch to go with you. You think you'll handle long distance?" She pulls a face insinuating that she doesn't.

"Of course, we will. This is us." Me and Cole have been together since we were thirteen, and there's nothing that can tear us apart.

"Long distance isn't for everyone; it might fade out," Zoe shrugs, taking another sip of her drink.

"Don't be ridiculous, we already have it planned. I'm gonna come home once a month, and he's gonna visit whenever he can. We'll make it work," I assure her, not liking the twist in my stomach that her words are causing.

"You really think you and him are for keeps? You've only ever known each other. What if you want to experiment?" I don't expect Zoe to understand; she gets itchy feet after a first date, for Christ's sake.

"I know we're for keeps. We talk about where we're gonna live and how many kids we'll have all the time." I shut her down, starting to get pissed off with her negativity.

"That's sweet." Zoe smiles unconvincingly.

"You don't believe in us, do you? You're just like my mom." Mom's always telling me Cole won't wait around for me. I swear it's her way to try to keep me here, herself. She's lonely now that Dad left her, and it's not like she's got Cole's mom, Teresa, around for company anymore. Most parents want their kids to go to college, but not her. She's too scared of being alone to encourage me to chase my dreams.

"I do. I'm just saying it's not gonna be easy. There are gonna be some hot-assed college boys in Washington that are gonna sweep you off your feet, and it's not like you two are committed to each other."

"What if we were committed?" I stand up as her words sink in. Me and Cole talk about our future all the time. I know he wants to marry me. Why do we have to wait until I get back? If I left here for Washington, his wife, it would prove to anyone who doubts us that what we have is real.

"Come on." I grab Zoe's car keys off the table and head for the door.

"Go where?" she giggles as she chases me out the house.

"I'm going to ask Cole Carson to marry me," I tell her over the roof of the car.

"Girl, you're talking crazy. You can't drive. You've been drinking, and in case you didn't realize, this is my car."

"Zoe, I hate to tell you this, but your margaritas are trash. I could barely taste the tequila." Zoe doesn't bother to argue, she just rolls her eyes at me again before getting in the passenger seat.

It's a twenty-minute ride from her place to the Copper Ridge Ranch, and I turn the stereo up so we can both sing at the top of our voices as I drive us through the back roads.

"So, what you gonna do when you get there? Just knock on the door and drop to your knee when he answers?" Zoe yells over the music.

"No, I'm not getting on my knees, that only happens when the guy does it." I focus on the road harder when the headlights coming toward us look blurry.

"And what about a ring? You can't propose without a ring," Zoe points out as the headlights get closer, and when I hear the loud honk of a horn, I realize that they're coming at us head-on. Zoe screams as I try to swerve out of the way, and when that scream gets silenced by the skidding of tires and shattering glass, I know we're in some real trouble.

"Wake up!" I feel my body shaking and my ears ringing. It takes me a while to open my eyes, and when I do, it's Mr. Mason's face

I see hanging over me. "Come on, we gotta get ya out of here." He slaps my face with his hand to snap me out of my trance before dragging my body to get me out of the car.

"Zoe," I somehow manage to twist my body and reach out to nudge her awake.

"She's gone." Mr. Mason continues to try and drag me away from her.

"No!" I fight against him, unclicking her safety belt and getting ready to drag her with us.

"Trust me, she's dead!" he yells at me, and when I look back at my friend and see the blood that's pouring out of her nose and the stillness of her eyes, I know he's telling the truth.

"No!" I scream hysterically, over and over again, until my throat becomes raw.

"Come on. I don't know if this is gonna go up." Mr. Mason tugs harder, taking me firmly under my arms and pulls me out.

"This is all my fault, she told me not to drive. I said I was ok. I've killed her!" I freak out, fighting against him to try and get to my friend. She can't be dead. Her life hasn't even started. She wants to go to Europe this summer.

"Why did she tell you not to drive?" Mr. Mason holds me by my shoulders and stares at me nervously.

"We'd been drinking, I was...I thought I was ok." I burst into tears, clutching my stomach and doubling over to try and scream out all the pain inside of me.

"Holy shit!" Mr. Mason sighs heavily, his eyes glancing up and down the road before he releases me and rushes back to the car.

"What are you doing? Do you think she might still be alive?" I get a little hope when he starts tugging her body across the console.

"Is she gonna be ok?" I ask, ignoring the pain in my ribs when I hobble over to see what he's doing.

"No!" he turns around and snaps.

"I checked her before I got to you. No pulse, no heartbeat. You see that huge gash on her forehead? That's probably from her head, hitting the dash at 60mph. She's dead alright, but you're not." He sets back to work, and when I see what he's doing, I stare at him in confusion.

"Why are you putting her there? Get her out." I shake my head when I see that he's placed her behind the wheel.

"The police are gonna be here soon, and if they know you were driving, you're gonna be in a whole heap of trouble. Sad as it is, that girl's life is already over. This is a small town, sweetheart. If folk around here know you're responsible for this, yours will be over, too," he tells me, and I sink to my knees and close my eyes. I always wondered if praying in church on a sunday was pointless. But I pray now. I pray that this is just a dream and that I'll wake up from it real soon.

"Get up." I flinch in pain when Mr. Mason drags me onto my feet. "You're gonna have to pull yourself together." He gets on the floor and pulls a Swiss Army Knife from his pocket, then lays back to reach under the car, and with both hands, he uses it to cut something.

"Get back." He shoos me away as he stands back up, pointing his head to the grass verge on the side of the road. Before I have a chance to ask him what he's doing, he backs toward me, striking a match and tossing it at the car. The explosion is almost instant, and I scream, racing to get to Zoe and colliding with Mr. Mason's chest. He holds me firmly in his arms and drags me to a safer distance, and I become too weak to fight. I become too weak to do anything.

"It's gonna be ok." I smell gasoline on the hand he strokes through my hair as I watch the flames grow higher and wonder to myself how I'm ever gonna live, knowing that this is all my fault.

. . .

Me and Ronnie Mason are the only people who know what really happened that night. He claims to have saved my life, but I disagree. Some days, having to live with the guilt makes me wish I'd died, too. For a while, I thought what I witnessed that night from Ronnie Mason was a rare act of kindness. I was wrong.

I never made it to college. Some days, I couldn't even make it out of bed. I struggled to get through each day because Zoe was on my mind 24/7. There was no one I could talk to, I was far too ashamed, and so I carried that guilt all alone. I stood at my friend's funeral and let her parents hug me. I listened to the rest of the town tell me I was blessed to still be alive when all I really wanted to do was die. Cole tried to make me better, but he didn't know the truth. If he did, I'd have lost him, too.

I felt like I was living in a world I didn't belong in until that one day when Ronnie Mason turned up at my door.

He decided it was time to use that act of kindness as leverage, and as much as I hated him for it, I saw it as a sign. Zoe died that night because of me; I took a whole life away from her. I sure didn't deserve to get the life I wanted. I was holding Cole back with my misery, tricking him into settling down with a girl he would never truly know because the girl he loved died that night in the car with Zoe. I knew me marrying Joe Mason would break his heart, but I figured it was better than the alternative. Cole loved the old me, the girl without secrets. Not the deceitful wreck I'd become.

I stand up and tuck the photo of us together in the back of my jeans, and sliding the bag that carries my money and a few spare clothes over my shoulder, I pick up the letter I wrote for Cole and head out the door.

The yard is empty, and all the wranglers, including Cole,

will be out moving the herd, but I still check for signs of anyone before I sneak into the bunkhouse.

I already know which bunk is Cole's. He told me he beat Wes at poker so he could have the single bed by the window that looks out toward mine and Joe's cabin. I lift up his pillow and kiss it before resting the letter on his mattress and placing it back down to cover it.

"I'm sorry," I whisper the words I wish I could say to him in person before I leave, and when I step back out into the yard with tears in my eyes and pain in my heart, I gasp when a firm hand grips my wrist and the bag, I'm carrying, is lifted off my shoulder.

"You going somewhere, sweetheart?" The voice makes me shiver, and when I look up into his cold eyes, I say another helpless prayer.

I wake up earlier than usual, and since Garrett is already up and at it, I decide to get back to cleaning up the mess in Mom and Breanna's bedrooms. I figure while I'm at it, I should box up some of Mom's things, and after a few hours, I have ten full boxes ready to go to charity. All Mom's clothes were designer, and I'm sure her jewelry is worth a fortune, too, but none of it feels sentimental. I don't want any of it. The woman was a leech, she made a fortune out of making men fall in love with her. Her being absent from my life for three years is sad, but it makes the fact I don't miss her understandable.

I head to the other side of the hall and get to work on Breanna's room. I could tell from the way Garrett looked around the mess yesterday that it brought him pain, and although I don't know where everything belongs, I can make it at least look tidy again. I pick up her clothes and hang them back up in the wardrobe. I stand everything that's been knocked sideways on her dressing table back up, and then I stack the books back on her bookshelf. I smile to myself when I notice the old worn copy of Pride and Prejudice; I remember back in high school I had to do an assignment on it for English Lit, and now I know where Darcy got her name from. I study the book a little harder, it's an old edition, probably worth some money, and when I open it up and read the message on the front page, I'm instantly intrigued.

Breanna
Love From
Your Fitzgerald

I read the words over and over and eventually recall that Fitgerald was the name of Mr. Darcy.

'Your Fitzgerald' indicates that whoever gave Breanna this book was romantically involved with her, and I wonder if it's a clue I could use as I slide the book back on the shelf and get back to work. It plays on my mind all morning, and when everything's straight again and I head down for lunch, I wonder if I should bring it up with Garrett.

I'm sitting at the kitchen counter, waiting for him, when he walks through the door, and I watch as he goes straight to the basin to wash his hands.

"Ya got that look on your face," he tells me with a slight smile on his lips.

"What kinda look?" I stand up and stalk toward him. He looks so handsome when he's dirty, it's hard to keep my hands to myself.

"The clever look ya get when you've done somethin' wrong."

"I haven't done anything wrong, not this time anyway," I assure him, reaching up to kiss him.

"Garrett!" Wade rushes into the kitchen. "Cole just called; he needs us."

"What's happened?" Garrett immediately pulls up his guard, his muscles tense and his eyebrows furrowed while he waits on Wade's explanation.

"It's Aubrey; she's missing. The Masons have organized a search to cover their ranch, but there's a lot of acres to cover."

"Have the boys load the horses," Garrett instructs him, already springing into action.

"Wait, what do you mean missing?" An unnerving hunch starts to creep inside me.

"I don't know, but Cole's freakin' the fuck out. All I got outta him was that no one's seen her since last night." Wade races off to give Garrett's instructions to the others, and I can tell by the look of concern on Garrett's face that he's worried, too.

"I want to come," I blurt out, staring up at him and warning him with my eyes not to challenge me.

"Maisie, the Mason Ranch is huge, and…"

"I'm coming," I talk over him. There's no way I'm staying here while they are all out searching. I have a bad feeling about this, a real bad feeling.

Garrett shakes his head and blows out a breath before grabbing my hand and dragging me out the door.

"Load up Darcy, too," he instructs Finn, who's already leading a disobedient Thunder toward the horse trailer when we pass him on the way to the truck. When we get there, Garrett doesn't open the door for me; instead he spins me around and pins me to it with his hips instead.

"You stay close to me, and if I tell ya to do somethin', ya don't question it." His finger points a warning at me, and I'm tempted to bite the end of it, but the seriousness of the situation holds me back.

"I promise," I whisper back at him, and seeming satisfied by my answer, he kisses my lips hard before he reaches around and opens the door for me.

When we get to the Mason's yard, the whole place is in

chaos, and I search among all the horses and riders that are saddled up ready to ride out, trying to seek out Cole.

"There he is," Garrett points his head over toward the corral where old man Mason is standing with an open map. He's pointing out his instructions and sending out teams, and Cole is staring at him like he wants him dead.

"Ronnie, we're here to help. I got Wade and three more of my men on their way with horses." Garrett speaks to old man Mason while I head over to Cole.

"You okay?" I keep my voice low, so I don't draw any attention.

"No, I ain't *o-fuckin'-kay!* No one's seen her since she came back from town yesterday." He doesn't take his glare off old man Mason while he speaks, and I can sense how on edge he is.

"And where's Joe?" I look around the yard and try to spot Aubrey's husband.

"He only got back from Utah a few hours ago, he's inside talkin' to Sheriff Nelson." I close my eyes and swallow down my guilt when I'm reminded that I may have caused all this.

"Maybe she needed to get out of town for a while, visit a friend. There could be a logical explanation for all this."

"She has no fuckin' friends, Maisie! She didn't take her car, she hasn't got a cell phone, and I'm pretty certain these fuckers have made sure she has no access to any money."

"Come on," Garrett interrupts us, "We're takin' the river on the North border. Wade, Finn, Tate and Mitch are backin' up around the woods." Right on cue, the horse lorry pulls up, and Wade rushes to his brother, not giving a shit that Ronnie Mason is standing right beside him.

"Don't worry, bro, we'll find her." He slaps Cole's shoulder enthusiastically, giving Mr. Mason a cold stare before he sets to work unloading the horses.

We ride along the river with Cole, our eyes searching for any clue that Aubrey has passed through this way.

"Is the rifle really necessary?" I ask Garrett. I noticed him slide it into his saddle sling before we left.

"Out here, a rifle is always necessary," he tells me, pulling Thunder to a halt when Cole, who's leading a little ahead of us, comes to a stand.

"You got somethin'?" Garrett calls out, and when Cole looks back at us over his shoulder, he looks nervous.

"I ain't got shit, but I keep wonderin' why ain't he out here lookin', too. He wasn't around last night, either."

"Joe Mason's never been one to get his hands dirty, you know that. Come on, we keep looking." Garrett clicks Thunder on.

"Ain't no horses missing from the stable, so wherever she went, she went on foot. How far could she have gotten, Garrett?" Cole questions helplessly before turning his horse and riding back toward the ranch.

"I need to speak to Joe," he tells us with his nostrils flaring and his eyes wild with rage.

"Cole, that's a bad idea, you're angry, and you're scared. Let's cover our ground, and then we'll go back. For all we know, she ain't even out here, she could've jumped on a bus and headed out of town. Let the police do their job checkin' the CCTV in town, and we'll do ours out here." Garrett tries talking some sense into him, but Cole shakes his head.

"What if he found out?" I feel the guilt I'm already carrying multiply when Cole suggests that.

"Cole, we keep looking." Garrett throws him a warning look and I look between the two brothers and wonder who's gonna win the stare-off.

"Fine." Cole surprises me when he eventually gives in, redirecting his horse and heading forward with us.

CHAPTER 22

GARRETT

We're at least three miles from the Mason Ranch now, and there's still no sign of Aubrey. I can see Maisie growing more and more worried while Cole gets more and more angry. I notice something upriver and hold my arm out to halt Maisie and Darcy. Cole has ridden much further ahead after moaning that she was slowing us down. I edge Thunder a little closer to the river, warning Maisie to stay back, and I hope to God, on this occasion, she fucking listens to me because what I think I'm seeing is liable to stay with her if she doesn't.

"Cole!" I call out my brother's name as I slide off Thunder's back and take the rest of the ground on foot.

"He can't hear you. What is it?" Maisie asks with a tremble in her voice.

I place two fingers in my mouth and whistle. "Cole!" I call out again, this time louder. What I'm seeing now is unmistakable. It's a body, and it ain't moving.

I quickly tie Thunder up to a tree and take the rough terrain steadily down toward it, and Cole suddenly appears, racing down the bank a little further upstream.

"Aubrey?" I don't know if it's hope or fear I hear in his voice, but whatever it is, I feel it deep in my chest.

"Garrett. What is it?" I look up and see Maisie peering down at me.

"Get back. Right now, Maisie!" I yell at her, holding up my arm like a barrier. "Please." I pray she doesn't argue, not now.

"*Aubrey!*" Cole's scream diverts my attention, and hoping that Maisie will heed my warning, I dodge the rocks and rush over to him.

"She's not movin', Garrett, and she's cold." Cole chokes on his breath as he strips out of his jacket and places it over her back, rubbing her hard and trying to warm her up, but the second he rolls her over, I know there ain't no hope for her.

"Cole. Step away from her," I warn, seeing that her face is beaten black and blue, and then noticing the rock that's covered in blood on the ground beside her.

I can't stand the fact that Cole's looking at me like he's expecting me to do something to fix this.

"She's gone." I place my hand on his shoulder, but he shoves it away.

"You're talkin' shit!" he barks at me, grabbing her body in his arms and dragging her on to his chest, and when her arm falls limp, he acts like he doesn't notice.

"Wake up, baby, come on." He taps her cheek with his hand, and when she makes no response, he looks up at the sky with tears filling his eyes.

"Cole, she's dead." I hate saying the words, and I hate the painful expression that creeps onto his face as he lets them sink in. He spares me from it when drops his head onto hers, and I watch his shoulders shake as he sobs.

I can't remember ever seeing Cole cry, not even when Mama left us or when we lost Breanna. I always thought he was lacking a lot when it came to emotion, and I envied him for it. What I'm seeing in front of me now is him ripping at the seams, and I'm not gonna pretend I ain't scared about what that might unleash.

I stand in silence for a while and watch him. He needs to

know I'm here for him whenever he's ready, and when he eventually looks up at me with red-rimmed eyes full of pain, I watch his nostrils flare as all that agony turns to rage. He stands up on his feet, lifting her up with him, and I shake my head.

"Cole, you can't move her, this is a crime scene. I'll call the sheriff."

"You won't get a signal for miles, and I ain't leavin' her out here." He shifts Aubrey's body higher, so she's cradled in his arms and then starts heading toward a less steep part of the bank. I watch him struggle to climb it, knowing he won't accept my help even if I offered it, and then I hear the loud sob Maisie makes when he reaches the top.

"No. Oh my God... No!" she screams in panic, and I race up the bank so I can try to comfort her.

"Come here, darlin'." I pull her close and hold her face tight to my chest to shield her from the sight of Aubrey's limp body in my brother's arms. I'm so grateful to feel her chest beating against mine, even if it's frantic, and it hurts too much to imagine how I'd feel right now if it was her. I'd tear the world apart, and as I watch my brother place Aubrey over his saddle, it unnerves me how calm he's being. He must be in some kinda shock.

Slowly he starts walking his horse back toward the ranch, and I let him get a good head start, knowing that he needs his space. We can catch up with him in a few minutes.

"Garrett, this is all my fault," Maisie cries, and I pull her head back and use my thumbs to wipe away her tears.

"None of this is your fault." I narrow my eyes at her. "We gotta be there for Cole," I warn, knowing that what comes next is gonna be tough. My brother loved that woman enough to stay working on a ranch where he was treated like shit and humiliated daily. He's never moved on because she was the person he was meant to be with. He held on to hope, and now all that hope is gone.

"I can do that." She catches her breath and nods at me bravely.

"That's my girl. Now get back on your horse, and let's go make sure he doesn't do anything stupid." I kiss her forehead.

When we catch up with Cole, I make sure we keep a few meters back. I can imagine some of the things that are going through his head and can only predict how he's gonna react when we get back to the Mason's yard. I try calling Wade and the others, but Cole was right; there's no reception out here.

"When we get back, I need ya to get straight in the truck," I tell Maisie, hoping that there will be someone there I can get to drive her straight home. I don't wanna to see, or be around, the shit storm I know is gonna go down.

"You can't let him do anything stupid, Garrett." My girl's eyes look so sad when she looks over at me.

"It's a little late for that," I tell her helplessly, reaching over to her saddle and taking her hand as we follow Cole through the paddock and onto the Mason's yard.

Joe and his father are on their porch, talking to Kerry Winters, she's a news reporter based in Billings, and I gotta feeling Cole's about to give her one hell of a story. There's loads of people gathered in the yard, and they part way for Cole as he passes straight through 'em with Aubrey's body hanging over his saddle. Joe Mason turns white when he sees what's coming toward him, and his father stands on his feet and shares the same startled look when Cole lifts Aubrey down and carries her in his arms toward the porch.

"Garrett," Maisie turns to look at me with concern, and we both watch as he places her down gently on the top of the steps by their feet. He keeps the stern look on his face as he raises back up, staring at them both like his eyes are made from steel.

"Ya happy now?" he asks calmly, and I tighten my grip on Maisie's hand as he slowly backs away from them. When he heads towards us, I see that bitterness in his eyes and know he's reached that point of no return.

He jumps back on his horse, tugging at his reins and trotting closer to us.

"I'm gonna kill 'em all," he utters under his breath at me before galloping off and leaving us to explain to everyone what happened.

"Hey, time to wake up." I feel a nudge, and when I open my eyes and see Garrett looking down on me, I smile. Then the reality of what happened yesterday hits me. We both had to give statements to Sheriff Nelson, and I stayed at the Mason Ranch with Tate and Finn guarding me like snarling dogs while Garrett took him out to the spot where we found Aubrey. I was there when the private ambulance came and took her away, and despite wanting to scream, I managed to remain silent.

Joe Mason paced his porch like a desperate, grieving husband, he even managed a few tears as they wheeled her away on the gurney, and as I watched him put on his display, I couldn't help hoping that whatever Cole has planned for him is brutal.

"Did Cole come home?" I ask, stretching out my arms and remembering how worried we all were when he didn't come back last night. There's no way he can stay at the Mason Ranch, not now. And seeing how mad he was when he left made me worry about what he might do.

"Yeah, Wade found him; they got back about three hours ago."

"He must have been out looking all night. You should have gone with him." I go to sit up, but Garrett eases me back down.

"I wanted to be here with you. What happened yesterday was a lot to take in."

"I'm fine. We should go be with Cole."

"Cole ain't in a good place right now, he needs his space," he explains, gently massaging his hand into my shoulder. "Besides, I have plans for us."

"What kinda plans?" I smile, wondering if they're the same as mine. I need a distraction from that horrible feeling in my gut that tells me all this is a result of my meddling.

"I need ya to get dressed, I'm takin' you to Billings for some lunch and then we're gonna get married." He pushes himself off the bed and heads over to his wardrobe, flicking through the hangers and pulling out the suit he wore to my mother's funeral.

"Did you say we're getting married?" I check I heard him right, and when he turns back around to face me, the casual way he nods his head has me confused.

"Give me a second to wake up here," I sit up on the bed and rub my temples. "Are you proposing to me?" As crazy as those words sound, I can't help smiling at them. Garrett hangs his suit on the front of his wardrobe and moves to sit on the mattress in front of me. When he takes my cheek in his hand, I notice that his eyes are much softer than usual, and the fact he's only wearing his jeans has me at a complete disadvantage to whatever argument he's going to put forward.

"No, darlin'. A proposal would mean you had a choice in the matter. I ain't *askin'* ya to marry me, I'm *insistin'* on it." That tiny little smirk that I've fallen in love with creeps onto his lips, and as much as I want to pounce on him and kiss it, I have to get my head straight.

"Garrett, you can't just wake up and decide to get married!" I watch him as he gets up and swaps his jeans for his suit pants, buckling up the belt he wears for special occasions.

"I didn't. I've had the license since I knew you were comin' back to town," he mentions matter-of-factly as he buttons up his shirt.

"What! How? I'm sure it takes two people to sign for a license, not to mention all the paperwork. Mom had to have a goddamn blood test when she married your father." I get out of bed and pace the floor in front of it, suddenly feeling very awake.

"Hey, come here." Garrett stands in front of me and holds me still. "Stop freakin' out."

"How am I supposed to not freak out? The guy I've been seeing a week just told me we're getting married, with some magically obtained license and…"

"And what?" He tilts his head and waits for me to give him another reason why this is a bad idea.

"And we can't." I hate saying no to him, especially since it's what I've been wanting for so long, but the timing isn't right.

"Garrett, your brother just lost the woman he's loved his whole life," I point out.

"Which is *exactly* why I've decided today has to be the day. I was gonna try and think up some fancy way to ask ya, but after what happened yesterday, I'm not wasting another day without ya bein' my wife. We'll go to the courthouse to get it legalized, and then we can have a blessing in the church and throw whatever kinda party ya want." His thumb trails over my bottom lip, and I almost get lost in the fantasy of it all.

"We can't, it's insensitive, and anyway, I'm not stealing Leia's thunder like that. She's been planning her wedding for months. What kinda friend would I be if I got married before her?" I shake my head because as much as I like the idea, it's just not plausible.

"First off, there ain't no one in the world right now that would understand me wantin' to do this more than Cole. Yes, he just lost the woman he loved, and he may be a hard bastard at times but trust me when I say he'll get it. Second of all, Leia's wedding is a complete sham, and you know it."

"Sham or not, it's her big day, and I won't ruin it. I'll marry you, Garrett Carson, but not today." I spin around, ready to get back into bed, but he drags me back, wrapping his hands around my thighs and lifting me onto his body.

"That wedding is months away! I ain't waiting that long," he tells me sternly.

"Ain't I worth the wait?" I widen my eyes.

"Oh, ya worth the wait, but I'm not holdin' out on knockin' you up, and I'd really like to get a ring on ya finger before that happens." I should be shocked by his answer, but I'm not.

"For all we know, it could have already happened," I shrug, thinking of all the times we've been together without using protection. I really have jumped into this feet first, but I'd dare anyone not to fall for this man and want to give him everything.

"With any luck." He knits his eyebrows together and confirms that it's been what he's wanted from the start.

"I'm not budging on this. I'm not getting married before Leia." I stand firm until he dips his head and makes a trail of kisses up my neck.

"Then how about a compromise?" he whispers into my ear.

"You look scared." Garrett's looking smug as we sit in the courthouse waiting room.

"I am. I've got a terrible feeling that I'm about to commit a crime." I keep my voice low so no one can hear. "You still haven't explained how you got this license. So, I'm assuming it's not legal." I study his face for a weakness but get nothing.

"The license is legal," he assures me, "How I obtained it,

not so much," he shrugs his shoulders and clears his throat when a member of staff steps out from behind the reception desk and passes us on her way to one of the offices.

"Garrett." I elbow him hard and watch the smile on his face grow wider. "Do you know what a contradiction that is?"

"You're here, ain't ya?" he tells me cockily.

"I got a good mind to walk out that door," I warn, and the low, growly laugh he makes as he leans into me has me squeezing my thighs together.

"Try it. See what happens," he warns, biting at my ear lobe before he pulls away.

"Mr. Carson and Miss. Wildman." The registrar comes to the door and calls us through; Garrett stands, buttoning up his suit jacket and holding out his hand for me.

"You ready?" he asks, curling his fingers around mine and pulling me onto my feet.

"You'll keep your promise?" I check, reminding him of the deal we made before we left the ranch.

"No one finds out until after Leia's big day," he assures me, then nods at the couple he dragged off the street to be our witnesses, to follow us.

I watch the new Mrs. Carson step toward the truck, and I just have to kiss her. Pulling her around and slamming her back against the passenger door, I kiss her lips hard and grip her jaw tight in my hand.

"Let me get that door for ya, Mrs. Carson," I tell her, trying to control the smug smile I'm wearing. She doesn't look much like a bride, but she's still fuckin' beautiful. She's wearing a short, floral dress with cowgirl boots and a denim jacket. The gold band on her finger, that used to be my grandma's, looks perfect there.

"You know I can't keep this on." She stretches out her hand and admires it as we're riding back toward Fork River.

"Sure ya can." I already don't like the idea of her taking it off, but I guess a promise is a promise.

"So, are you gonna tell me how you got the license?" she changes the subject. "And while you're at it, you can tell me how you got those shares transferred into my name without me knowing, too."

I still can't understand why I love it so much when she gets bossy.

"You remember Miles?" I ask, taking my eyes off the road to look at her again. It's hard to believe that after all this time, she's actually mine.

"The dodgy lawyer who gets you off murder charges? Sure, I remember him," she sniggers.

"Well, he handled the shares. A signature isn't hard to forge."

"And the license?" She pushes for more.

"That was more complicated. I had to call in an outside source for that one." I don't wanna get into my uncle and the biker gang he runs with her right now; she already knows that she hasn't married a law-abiding man, but I don't wanna scare her off completely.

"What kind of outside source?" She has an intrigued look on her face now, and when she shimmies across the bench seat to be closer to me, I take one hand off the wheel and wrap it around her shoulder.

"I gotta uncle in Colorado who knows a girl who can do all kinds of shit with a computer; gettin' that license was a five-minute job for her," I explain.

"Well, I'm glad you did it. Crazy as all this is, I like being Mrs. Carson." She kisses my cheek, and it warms the whole of my body because I like it a whole lot, too.

When we get back to the ranch, I rush around the truck to open her door for her, and checking around the yard for anyone watching, I lift her out and carry her toward the porch.

"What are you doing?" She tucks her head into my neck, and her giggles tickle my skin.

"I'm carrying my wife over the threshold," I explain, and she quickly hushes me by pressing her finger over my lips.

"Our secret, remember?" she reminds me and I nod my head and manage to open the door before carrying her toward the stairs.

"Where are we going?" She laughs as I start taking the steps upstairs.

"To get started on all those babies we're gonna make." It's a relief that she knows where I am with this now. It felt kinda deceitful before. But just lately, I've become obsessed with the idea.

I kick open my door and lay my wife out on the mattress. I've already decided that the cute, cowgirl boots she's wearing are staying on for sure, and I watch the seductive, little smile pull on her lips when I reach under her dress and pull her panties down her legs. I maneuver them over her boots and throw them aside, then scrunching up that pretty, little dress in my fist, I push it up her body and place my head between her thighs. I kiss her pussy lips and flick her with my tongue, tasting her as she gets wetter for me.

Maisie makes the sweetest sounds when she's satisfied, and when I slide a finger inside her, she moans even louder. I've never studied the art of babymaking before, but I figure the softer I can make her pussy, the better the chances. I shrug outta my suit jacket and loosen my pants before climbing up her body and letting my cock rub against her sensitive flesh. I absorb every expression she makes as she takes pleasure in it, and when it naturally finds its way to her entrance, I feel the heel of those boots she's wearing dig into my ass as she coaxes me deeper.

"I wanna give ya the world, Maisie Carson." I collapse over her when she's full of me, and I love the way her eyes still water a little whenever she takes it.

"You already have." Grabbing at my shirt, she pulls me down onto her lips and releases those tiny, little moans into my mouth as I thrust in and out of her, cradling her jaw and making sure I've got all the attention of her pretty, blue eyes. It doesn't take her long to come, which is good because knowing she's mine and that nothing can take her away from me now has me edging real close to finishing myself. Her body goes tense, and she squeezes at my chest as I pump inside her, deep and hard, gripping at the long, blonde hair she's got fanned over the mattress as I fill her pussy with cum.

"Is *now* a good time to tell ya that I love ya?" I ask, wondering if I'll always feel that niggle of pain that comes with it.

"It's the perfect time." Her finger traces over the 'CR' on my chest before she looks up at me again.

"I love you." I narrow my eyes at her to make sure she knows I mean every word.

"And I love you, too." That cute smile shines back at me, and I have to kiss it to believe that it's real.

"Garrett." The door bangs, and I drop my head into her shoulder.

"I swear to god I'm gonna castrate him." Sliding out of her, I pull up the pants from around my ankles and wait for her to straighten up before I open the door.

"Sorry to interrupt ya, but Sheriff Nelson's downstairs," Wade tells me, looking over my shoulder and raising his hat at Maisie. She quickly sits on her hand, worrying that he might notice the ring.

"Tell him I'll be down in a minute."

"It's actually Cole, he came to see, but I figured it was best you be there. Cole's a little hot-headed right now." Wade chews the side of his cheek, and it brings me back down to earth with a thump when I see how worried he is.

"Gimme five," I explain, turning around to face Maisie.

"And *you*, stay right there." I point my finger at her before heading for my sister's room.

I return a few minutes later and see that Maisie's done as she's told.

"Gimme the ring." I hold out my palm to her, and she stares at it, confused.

"You wanna take it back already?" She looks up at me cleverly as she slides it from her finger and places it in my hand.

"No, I don't ever want ya takin' it off, so I've come up with another compromise."

Taking the thin golden chain from my pocket, I thread the ring onto it and hold it in front of her.

"This was Breanna's. I bought it for her sixteenth birthday." Climbing onto the bed behind her, I hang the necklace in front of her, and she sweeps her hair to the side so I can fasten it around her neck. "I think she would've wanted ya to have it." I kiss her shoulder before I pull away, ready to go downstairs and face Sheriff Nelson. Maisie turns to look at me, clutching the ring and chain tight in her fist against her chest.

"You're a beautiful man, you know that? And not just on the outside. On the inside, too." She looks so happy as she leaps onto me and squeezes me tight. And as good as it feels, I can't help wondering if she would still believe that if she knew all the things I'd done and the things I'm prepared to do because seeing her this happy has only confirmed that there really *are* no limits to how far I'd go.

I leave Maisie in our room and head downstairs, where I find Cole, Wade and Sheriff Nelson in the living room. Cole looks furious, with his eyes staring at the floor, we've hardly got a word outta him since we found Aubrey, and I can't imagine the pain he must be in.

"What can we do for ya, Sheriff?" I head to the drinks cabinet, yeah, it's early, but it ain't every day a man gets the woman he loves to marry him, and it ain't every day a man loses his, the way Cole has. I pour for me and both my brothers, and when I offer one to Nelson, he shakes his head and refuses.

"I need Cole to come to the station so we can take his fingerprints," he informs us.

"Is that really necessary?" I remain calm as I take a sip of my scotch.

"Aubrey Mason was murdered," Nelson tells us something we already figured, "I gotta rule out all eventualities, especially with Swann crawling around. Two murders within such a small timescale, she's trying to link them," he explains, looking exhausted.

"We all know who killed her. She came to the station to give me an alibi, and within 24 hours, she's found dead. It don't take a fuckin' detective to figure it out." Cole lifts his eyes from the floor and pins Nelson with 'em.

"I know it weren't you, Cole, but this ain't my request. Just come, give me the prints and let 'em figure it out."

"That's the problem, though. I don't want 'em to figure it out. I wanna kill that fucker myself, and I warn you all, I won't give a shit if I go down for the pleasure." Cole knocks his drink back and slams his glass on the coffee table.

"We have Mr. Mason in custody, he's being questioned," Nelson informs us.

"Well, ain't that just great?" Cole stands up and steps into his face.

"Come on, now," Wade puts his arm between them, but Cole ain't backing down.

"That man needs to pay for what he did, and prison would be far too kind."

"Like I said, it's outta my hands." Sheriff Nelson holds firm, showing that he ain't afraid of my brother.

"I'll bring him into the station myself," I assure Nelson, moving calmly toward them and steadily urging the sheriff out the door. I wait till he's in his patroller before I slam it shut and charge at my brother.

"Cole, I get you're in pain, but ya gotta be smarter," I warn him, scrubbing my hand over my face before I go to the bar to pour myself another drink.

"She's fuckin' dead, Garrett, and we all know who did it!" my brother yells across the room at me, and Wade takes a seat, keeping his head low.

"Yeah, we do, we all know, but he's under police surveillance, and I will *not* have ya go to prison for that weasel. D'ya hear me?"

"I don't know if this is the time..." Wade leans forward and takes an envelope from his back pocket, handing it over to Cole.

"I went to the ranch this mornin' to clear your bunk since I figured ya wouldn't be goin' back. I found this under your pillow."

Cole stares at the envelope in his hand and swallows thickly.

"That's Aubrey's handwriting." His voice comes out weak, and when he slumps into the chair behind him, I notice his hands trembling as he rips it open.

I look across the room to Wade, and we both share the same sadness as we stand in silence and watch our brother's eyes fill up with tears as he scans them across the letter.

"This just proves it." He lays the letter out on the coffee table when he's done, sitting back in his seat and running his finger over his bottom lip.

"You mind if I...?" I reach for the letter, and Cole nods his permission before I pick it up.

Cole,

I don't know how to start this, it feels impossible to put it into words. Especially ones that I can expect you to understand. So, I'll get straight to it.

I'm leaving Fork River, I'm leaving Joe, and as much as it breaks my heart, I'm leaving you, too.

For so long, I've held on to a secret, one that pathed the route to our heartache and led us here. I don't expect your forgiveness for what I've put us through. I don't deserve that, but what you deserve is an explanation.

The night Zoe died; I was on my way to your house to ask you if you'd marry me. Yes, we were only seventeen, and yes, I was being crazy, but the thought of leaving you and going to college without committing to being yours made me not wanna leave at all. Me and Zoe had both been drinking that night, and it was me that got behind the wheel. I thought I was okay, but I couldn't have been because I ran us off the road.

Ronnie Mason was the first person there, he dragged me out the car, and when he figured Zoe was already dead, he came up with the plan to put her in the driving seat.

I wish now that I'd refused because at least that way, I could have suffered the guilt openly. Instead, I lived in the shadow of a lie. I couldn't tell you because I feared I'd lose you, and I always loved the way you'd look at me like I was perfect.

I was already broken when Ronnie came to me a year later to call in the favor he decided that I owed him, so by then, I was already feeling guilty for having my life when she didn't. It felt like justice that I would live the rest of it without love. So, I went along with his demands, and I married Joe.

I proved how selfish I am by spending these past eighteen months with you, reminding us of all we lost and how it might have been. But now I gotta leave the past behind, and I have to leave you with it, because you deserve better than what I am.

Please don't try to find me. I'm not the girl you fell in love with all those years ago, and I'm not the woman you think you lost.

Not everyone gets their happy ever after, but the time we had before the world turned gray, was the closest I ever got.

Yours always,

Aubrey.

. . .

"Shit," I pass the letter to Wade and pick up Cole's glass so I can top him up.

"That son of a bitch blackmailed her." Cole stares at an empty space on the floor and shakes his head. "She was leaving him, and they decided she had to be stopped."

"We'll make 'em pay," I promise, and I mean it. Everyone in town knows that Ronnie Mason is a cunt, but he's a cunt with a lot of money, and he has all the right connections. I was limited on how much I could progress, with Cora hanging in the wings waiting for me to fuck up. But Cora ain't here now, and my brother's hurting. If killing those assholes is what it's gonna take to make that hurt go away, then that's what has to happen.

My cell starts to ring, and when I see Sheriff Nelson's name, I immediately pick it up.

"I'm just giving you heads up, just got a call from Swann. They've released Joe Mason."

"What?" I hiss down the line. At least having that fucker behind bars for a while would've allowed me some time to think through his execution. Knowing he's free is gonna send Cole gung-ho.

"He's got an alibi for the time of death the coroner gave us."

"Who?" I clutch my cell tighter in my hand.

"Some wrangler who works for him, Laurie Cross," he admits sounding deflated.

"Surely that ain't solid, he works for him, for Christ's sake, and Laurie Cross is a professional bullshitter."

"Like I said..."

"Outta ya fuckin' hands." I finish his sentence for him and hang up, tossing my cell at the couch and heading for the bar, this time to pour *me* a fucking drink.

"What he say?" Cole asks, and I take a few seconds to brace myself before I tell him.

"They released Joe. Apparently he got an alibi." I knock back my scotch.

"Must be my lucky day." Cole stares at me coldly as he gets up from the chair and heads for the office. I march after him knowing exactly where he's heading.

"Stop!" I race around him and block him from getting to the gun cabinet.

"I agree Joe Mason needs to die, but I will not have you thrown in jail for it. We've put plenty of men under, but we never get caught, and ya know why we never get caught?" I point my finger in his face and show some authority in the hope it will back him down. "Because we're smart about it."

"Who's the alibi?" he asks with furious tears flooding his eyes.

"Laurie Cross," I speak the name of one of the few men who betrayed us and lived to tell the tale. He remained alive because he had a purpose, but that's no longer the case.

"Give me one good reason why I shouldn't blow every one of the Mason's heads off?" Cole tenses his jaw and waits for me to answer.

"Because we're smarter than that, we're smarter than them, and if ya do that, none of 'em gets to really suffer." I watch his shoulders sag as he takes in what I say, he's breathing like a bull, and I can feel his frustration, but he knows I'm right.

"So, whatcha suggest?" he asks.

"Wade, call a meeting. I want every branded man at the long camp for 8pm," I nod in my other brother's direction.

"And I want Laurie Cross there, too." Turning my head back to Cole, I smile at him darkly. "Let's start off with a little one, shall we?"

CHAPTER 25

MAISIE

I'm standing on the porch around the back of the house, watching the orange sky as the sun sets over the mountains, when Garrett steps up behind me. He places a glass of wine in my hand before draping a blanket over my shoulders and wrapping me up in his arms.

"If I didn't know better, I'd say you were sucking up to me." I keep looking out at the bright, orange sky as he rests his chin on my shoulder and admires it with me.

"I gotta head out for a few hours later," he admits, squeezing his arms a little tighter around my waist like he's expecting me to bolt.

"D'ya mind?"

"Is it for Cole?" I ask. Everyone's been cagey since Sheriff Nelson left, and I still haven't seen Cole. Both Wade and Garrett have assured me that he's better off alone, but I hate the thought of him having no one with him while he grieves.

"Yeah, darlin', it's for Cole," he whispers, sliding his nose up my cheek and kissing my temple. I love it when Garrett is gentle, especially when I know how brutal he can be.

"Then I don't mind at all." I balance my glass on the wooden rail in front of me and turn around, wrapping my arms around his neck.

"Hardly a way for a bride to spend her wedding night, though." He looks disappointed in himself, and I hate it. I never want him to feel torn between me and his brothers. Way I see it, earlier today, I married into this family, and just like they do, I'll fight to keep us together. I wasn't raised to have family values, my mom was barely ever around, and my father figure was whoever she was conning at the time, maybe that's why I want all this so badly now.

"I'm sure you'll make it up to me." I lick my lips seductively before I kiss him, and when he pulls away from me and smiles, I can tell he's already got something planned.

"I called Leia, she's on her way over to keep ya company."

Just when I don't think I can fall any harder for this man, he proves again how thoughtful he is. It's been an overwhelming few days, and although I'm not gonna tell her about the wedding, it'll be nice to talk about some of the other events with Leia. I noticed yesterday at the Mason Ranch how out of place she looked. Leia is fun and full of life, her parents may be rich and have a reputation to uphold, but they embrace her personality. The Masons have different values, and seeing what's happened to Aubrey makes me even more determined to make my friend see sense.

"I made sure Josie stocked up on wine; there's plenty in the fridge, and Leia's bringin' over pizza," he assures me.

"You hate pizza," I remind him.

"I ain't eatin' it. I'll grab something before I leave. So... d'ya forgive me for abandoning ya on our wedding night?" he checks, looking as if my answer really matters to him.

"You're making a good start." I let him know it's ok by kissing him again.

"What you two plottin'?" Wade steps out to join us, lighting himself a cigarette and looking out at the view.

"Shit, I'm sorry. Did I ruin a moment or summat." he laughs and makes us chuckle, too. Though all our faces turn serious again when we notice Cole riding in toward the yard.

"You guys need to be there for him," I tell them both

something they probably already know. "I've learnt real quick that Carson men are shit when it comes to asking for help." I pick up my wine glass and kiss my husband on his cheek, then I kiss Wade on his, too, before I head back into the house and prepare for Leia.

"Caleb swears it wasn't Joe, Maisie, and now this alibi proves it." Leia tops up her glass and joins me on the couch, I decided it would be fun for us to hang out at the studio tonight, and I think Garrett is being way overcautious by insisting that Otis sit guard downstairs. Still, I didn't argue with him, he's got enough on his mind without me acting like a brat.

"Of course, he's gonna say that; he's his brother," I point out, not buying the Masons' bullshit. I saw how scared Aubrey was of her husband. "There's something off. Who else would want her dead? You saw the way she was, always looking at the floor, she feared him. It's too coincidental. Garrett tells me this guy who says he was with him, works on the ranch; he could have been paid to say Joe was with him."

"Don't you think you should be focusing on solving a different murder?" I don't know if the look Leia's giving me is sympathetic or judgmental, but either way, I don't like it.

"I'd rather focus on the people I care about, besides, how do we know Joe didn't kill my mom, too? He's got the serial killer look about him," I sip my wine and shrug.

"You really have a crazy imagination." Leia rolls her eyes.

"Seriously Leia, aren't you worried about marrying into all of that? Don't you look at Aubrey and worry that it's what *you* might become." I'm taking a risk here, the last thing I want to do is push my friend away, but I have to get her to think this through.

"Me and Caleb make sense." Her answer isn't convincing at all, and the way she shifts in her seat uncomfortably makes me feel bad for the fact I'm not gonna let her get out of this conversation we're about to have.

"You're marrying him because it makes *sense*?" Now it's time for me to look judgy.

"Jesus, Maisie, you've been back in town five minutes, you really gonna start meddling?"

"If meddling is what it takes to ensure my best friend is happy, then yes. I'm meddling." We both laugh, and at least it shows that I haven't offended her.

"Look, me and Caleb, we both had the same kinda upbringing, we have ambitious parents, and we just kinda fit. Not all couples have it the way you and Garrett do." She nudges me playfully to try and distract me from the sadness in her eyes.

"But what if you could have that? What if there was this guy, someone real close, who had these raw, overwhelming feelings for you that he couldn't control but is just too scared to admit it?" I try putting it into words, but she bursts out laughing again.

"Maisie Wildman, you are reading far too many romance novels."

"I'm being serious here, what if you, settling for Caleb because it '*makes sense*'," I air quote her with my fingers, "stops you from finding real love?"

"Maisie, darling, I'm gonna let you into a little secret," Leia leans in closer and whispers, "real love, it don't exist."

I touch the chain around my neck, and I have to disagree with her. I felt the pain of real love for three years, and now I'm feeling the good of it.

"I disagree," I argue. "And if you marry Caleb Mason, you're denying yourself it."

"With who?" she laughs at me. "Maisie, I've had my fair share of boyfriends, and they're all assholes. When you get born into money and power, no one really sees you beyond that."

"But what if someone did? What if someone loved you for the way you smile or the way you make them laugh?"

"Someone like who?" she shakes her head to mock me as she reaches for another slice of pizza.

"I don't know, someone like Wade." I blurt out and have to quickly find a way to recover. "You know, just as an example."

"Wade?" Now she's really laughing. In fact she's almost doubled over.

"Wade, the kid who put a frog down my bathing suit when we went swimming in the lake as kids? The guy who grew up tugging on my pigtails and putting spiders in my lunch bag?"

"No, I'm talking about the Wade, who nearly smashed the brains out of Tyler Phillips on your daddy's fountain when he put something in your drink," I point out very fucking seriously, in the hope that she might finally get it.

"Me and Wade, we ain't like that. He's always been there for me, it's just his way." She smiles at me sadly, and every instinct inside me wants to tell her she's wrong.

"Anyway, enough about my love life. I want you to tell me all about yours." She wiggles her eyebrows excitedly.

"There's nothing to tell." I feel awful lying to her, but I'm not ready for people to know about the wedding yet. They wouldn't understand. And I know how much this wedding means to Leia, even if it isn't with a guy she loves.

"Lies!" she accuses me with a scowl, and just when I think she's caught me out, she smiles. "Everyone in Fork River were talking about how it must have been Garrett who killed your mom, and now all they're talking about is you."

"Me, what did I do?"

"You put a smile on his face, and that's a rare thing, trust me."

The idea of that makes me real happy, so happy that my chest feels like it might explode, and then suddenly, I feel guilty.

"I shouldn't feel so happy, not after what happened to Aubrey." I drop my eyes to my glass, ashamed of myself when I think about the letter Garrett showed me earlier. It certainly explained a lot.

"Stop that shit right now. You deserve to be happy. Sing it from the rooftop, girl." Leia looks genuinely pleased for me.

I wonder if she'd think that if she knew I was the one who made Aubrey change her statement, but to tell Leia that, I'd have to uncover a secret that isn't mine to share.

"I want to know everything there is to know about Garrett Carson and his moves." She smiles devilishly over the top of her wine glass.

"He doesn't have any moves." I shake my head.

"Oh yeah, so what were the two of you doing in the bathroom the night of my engagement party? Sawyer West tells me you came out looking very flustered."

"Ok, maybe he has *some* moves." I try hiding my smirk, but my cheeks ache too much, and when I finally give up and divulge a few secrets of my own, I make my new best friend blush.

CHAPTER 26

GARRETT

"So, what's ya thoughts?" I ask Noah after Sawyer and Zayne follow Mitch into the cabin to get a beer.

"You wanna know my thoughts?" The kid almost seems surprised. I can't figure out why. He's intelligent and does a lot of standing back and observing. He may have only been in town for five years, but I'm pretty sure he's got everybody figured.

"Cora, now Aubrey, you think it's related?" I toke back on my cigarette and stare at the fire in front of us.

"Can't see why Joe would wanna knock off Cora." He curls up his lip and shrugs, "But then stranger things have happened, especially in this town."

"You guys knew my sister; d'ya think Joe could've been the one who got her into trouble?" The thought makes my blood burn under my skin. Breanna was so young, barely even sixteen when she died. It's been hard enough imagining a guy her own age getting her pregnant, but a fully grown man..."

"I think those Mason men are capable of just about anything," Noah sighs, taking the beer Sawyer passes over his shoulder when he returns.

"So, what's the plan for Cross?" Sawyer asks, sitting himself next to Zayne, who's started rolling up a blunt.

"He's claiming he was with Joe at the time Aubrey was killed. We need to find out if that's true."

"And if it ain't? Last time I checked, you weren't into

beating the crap out of innocent men." Zayne looks up from what he's doing to raise his eyebrow.

"Laurie Cross ain't innocent; he stole from us a few years ago."

"And he's still breathin'?" Sawyer chuckles.

"He's had a purpose. I put him to work at the Mason Ranch so I could stay updated."

"Cole worked there, surely if ya needed to know somethin'..."

"Masons weren't gonna ever tell my brother shit. They only kept him employed so they could humiliate him," I interrupt him, reminding myself of how hard it must've been for him. Cole has always had a way of making things hard for himself.

"I'll bet Ronnie Mason got a hard-on over that shit," Mitch pitches in from over the other side of the fire, "and speak of the devil." His head tips toward the headlights when Cole's truck pulls up. When he gets out and slams the door, I see that all that rage and hurt is still with him. Scary truth is, I can't see it ever going away now. Cole's proven how much he loved Aubrey by his persistence to stay at the Mason's ranch. He was never gonna move on from her. I can't see the fact she's dead changing that.

"You got him?" he asks, taking a seat on the log beside Mitch.

"Dalton, Finn and Tate are on their way back with him now," I assure him.

"I'll getcha a beer." Mitch goes to stand up, but Cole shakes his head,

"I wanna straight head for this."

"We takin' it all the way?" Zayne lights the end of his blunt, sucking back hard to get it started.

"Don't see any use for him now," Cole clicks his knuckles and focuses on the flames that lick the air between us.

"He's a father," I remind them all. That fact has been playing on my mind all afternoon.

"And so are half the men you've put in the ground. What's ya point?" Cole snaps back at me.

"My point is, his kids are still young, and he may be a useless sack of shit, but those kids shouldn't have to suffer for it."

"Be doin' 'em a favor if you ask me," Noah stands up and feeds another log onto the fire. I gather from the sting in his tone that he never had much of a relationship with his father. No one really knows anything about who he was before he came here, but I can almost guarantee that he had it hard.

Wade's the next one to show up. He parks his truck beside Cole's and heads over, grabbing our brother by the shoulders and giving them a shake.

"You good?" he checks, and when Cole nods his head, it convinces no one.

It's another half an hour before more headlights appear in the distance, and all six of us stand up and wait to greet our guest.

Finn gets out of the black van first, opening the back doors, and Laurie Cross bolts outta them like a startled pony. Unfortunately for Lance he runs straight into Wade, who spears him to the ground, then stands him up to face us.

"Jesus, Finn, why the fuck is he naked?" My brother don't look impressed as he strains to keep Laurie still.

"Had to pull him outta the shower," Finn shrugs with a hint of amusement on his face.

"You three went to the Mason's bunkhouse?" Mitch knits his brows together.

"Nah, we asked around and found out that Laurie here, is a regular at the motel out on the 310. Like to spend all your hard-earned cash on a nasty little whore, don't cha?" Finn ruffles up Laurie's hair making him scowl.

"I thought she was alright," Dalton pipes up, and Tate rolls his eyes as he slams the van doors shut.

"You take care of the whore?" I step over and check,

"Gave her a hundred," he assures me, lighting up a cigarette and resting his shoulder against the side panel. "Dalton here wanted to give her hella lot more, though." His lips raise ever so slightly, before I turn around and face the man we need to speak to.

Usually this is where I'd take the lead, but this is Cole's party.

"I ain't got much tolerance, so I'm gonna ask ya this once, and I wanna straight answer. Are ya lying about being with Joe Mason while his wife was gettin' murdered?" Cole asks. He's trying to keep his cool, but I can hear the tension in his voice.

Laurie swallows hard as he glances around the circle we've formed around him.

"Yeah." He drops his eyes to the floor in shame, and Cole takes out his revolver and without any warning, shoots him straight between the legs. Wade lets Laurie drop to the floor so he can clutch his nutsack and scream in agony. Apart from Cole, who looks unapologetic, there ain't a man standing who doesn't have a cringe on his face.

Cole crouches down in front of Laurie watching him squirm.

"My brother here, says I'm not allowed to kill ya because ya got young un's. I just wanted to ensure ya don't have anymore."

"You son of a bitch!" Phlegm flies out of Laurie's mouth, and Cole laughs a cold, sadistic laugh that shows how unpredictable he can be.

"Get him on his feet." He stands back so Dalton and Sawyer

can set to work, lifting Laurie from under his armpits and holding him up. It gives us a full view of the mess Cole's made of his junk, and I ain't seen much faze Zayne, but he looks away and gags when he sees that his left nut is completely obliterated.

"I'll ask that question again. Were you with Joe Mason when his wife died?"

Laurie looks like he's about to pass out from the pain, and when his head flops forward, Cole shoves his gun up under his chin to push it back up. Laurie looks down at the barrel with pure terror in his eyes.

"I forgot to tell ya; I don't always listen to what my brother tells me," Cole warns. When Wade throws me a look that asks if he should step in, I shake my head subtly back at him and take a steady breath.

"No, I wasn't," Laurie confesses, and Cole pulls the gun away, taking a step back and firing it at Laurie's feet. It makes him dance, and the fucker screams like a baby before he falls back down on his knees.

"There's ya fuckin' answer." Cole puts his gun back in his holster and shoves past me, getting into his truck.

"We'll just take care of this!" Wade shouts after him sarcastically, and when I gesture my head for him to follow our brother to check he don't do anything stupid, he quickly races after him. Despite Cole protesting, Wade gets in the passenger seat, and they skid off.

"Whatcha want done with him, boss?" Dalton asks, staring at the broken man on the floor with what looks a lot like sympathy. I ignore him, stepping toward Laurie and lowering to his level.

"Your still breathing because of those two young boys of yours. I've given ya plenty of chances to do better." I keep my voice low and watch his eyes lose their fight. The fact he ain't screaming anymore tells me his body's gone into shock from all the pain he must be in.

"Fuck up again, and they won't be enough to protect you." I stand back up and head toward Sawyer.

"Ya think your Gran can handle this? If we drop him at the hospital, chances are, he's gonna squeak."

"She'll take care of it," he assures me, nodding his head toward Zayne to help him load the lying asshole into his truck. Mitch talks with Finn, Tate, and Dalton, no doubt checking that they covered all bases back at the motel, and Noah comes to me.

"D'ya want me to have Sheriff Nelson call by when he's in a better way? I'm guessin' you'll want him to make a new statement."

"That's the last thing I want" I tell him, taking another cigarette out from my jacket and lighting it up. The kid looks confused, and since branded men don't keep things from each other, I clue him in.

"If Laurie changes his statement, the police will arrest Joe again, and Cole is gonna struggle to get to him if he's behind bars."

Noah nods like he understands my logic.

"We've made some hits these past few years, but Joe Mason's a big one," he points out something I already know.

"How big he is don't matter, ain't nothin' I can do to stop Cole from killing him, ain't nothin' that would stop me either if that was my girl we found by the river."

"Ya know where we are if ya need us." Noah slaps my shoulder before heading off to join his buddies.

"Well, that was short and sweet." Mitch sniggers as he taps the van and sends the rest of the boys off.

"Hoping for more action?" I laugh at him, taking a seat on the log by the fire and drawing back on my cigarette.

"We're gonna have to keep an eye on that brother of yours, make sure he doesn't lose his head." He sounds concerned and looks very fucking serious.

"I think you and I both know Cole lost his head a long time ago." I try and make light of it, but the words I speak are true. Cole ain't been right since Mama left. I guess he struggled with the fact they were so close, and she abandoned him without any explanation. It all happened so close to the time my grandfather hung himself. I found it hard to accept myself.

I felt deceived, too. I just refused to let it destroy me.

"I'll keep him in check, in the meantime, be ready," I tell Mitch, standing back up and heading toward my truck. Since Cole wasted no time, I figure I can give my wife that wedding night after all.

L eia had to leave when her sister called her for a ride, and since it's still early, I decide to stay in my studio and finish the bottle of wine we opened. It seems like forever since I last painted anything and being out here might inspire me to come up with my next project. I lay my head on the back of the couch and look up at the soft, warm fairy lights that are wrapped around the beams. Thinking about Garrett doing all this for me makes me smile, and when I stand up and walk to the window looking out at the bright, starry night, it makes me wonder what it is he's doing tonight.

This place really is paradise. I never saw that when I first came here. I was too busy feeling sorry for myself, but now I understand why Garrett works so hard to keep it and the lengths he'll go to to protect it. I touch the blank canvas that's resting on the easel, hoping to visualize what I'm going to paint. The landscape is so beautiful; I figure it would be nice to take it into the house. We could hang it in the living room; I'm sure Garrett wouldn't mind, he's always reminding me that this place is my home now.

I hear the stairs creak and expect to see Otis when I spin around, but instead, it's Garrett who's got his arms resting on the top rail while he watches me.

"How long have you been there?" I smile.

"Long enough." He grins back at me.

"And how did you know I was out here?" I rush over to kiss him because, as pathetic as it sounds, it feels like we've been apart too long.

"I saw the lights on." The way he cradles my head in his hand so gently almost makes me not want to ask my next question, but I'm curious by nature.

"How did it go?" I smile, hoping it will let him know that however bad it is, he can share it with me.

"You really wanna know?" Stepping around me, he takes a seat on the couch that's facing out toward the stars and taps his lap for me to sit.

"Yeah, you know I don't want us to have secrets." I curl up on his lap and kiss his stubbly jaw.

"Laurie lied about being Joe's alibi," he informs me, letting out a long, exhausted breath.

"How do you know that?" I pull back in shock.

"'Cause we just had a conversation with Laurie Cross," he explains, taking off his hat and placing it on the seat beside us.

"What kind of a conversation?" I bite my lip and glance down to check Garrett's hands; they seem clean enough.

"The kind that had Cole blowin' off his left nut." If he didn't have such a serious look on his face, I'd think he was kidding.

"Holy crap." I take a steady breath and close my eyes.

"Hey, you're the one who wants no secrets." He holds up his hands in defense. "Around here the truth can get real ugly." He smiles sadly.

"Where's Leia?" he looks around like he's only just realized she's not here.

"She had to go pick up Karina from a party. So, I stayed out here to get some inspiration. I did tell Otis he could leave, but he insisted on staying down there on guard."

"That's because he's sensible," Garrett tells me, and as much as it worries me that he feels the need to keep me guarded, I decide to not let it show.

"I'm thinking of painting the view so we can hang it in the living room." I change the subject, nestling my head into his neck and taking his hand in mine so I can play with his fingers.

"Ya like it up here?" he asks after a few minutes of silence.

"I love it. I love even more that you did it for me before I even came back," I admit, running my fingers over the scabs and scars on his hands.

"I had to, a man's gotta have some hope."

"You could have just called." I look up at him through my lashes, and when he gives me a stern frown, I laugh.

"You wanna know what inspired me to do this?" he asks in that low, gravelly voice that pulls at my insides.

"Of course, I do." Garrett's a closed book, you can never be sure what's going on in his head, so getting a glimpse inside it sounds appealing.

"I had a vision." He swipes his thumb over my bottom lip and stares deep into my eyes.

"A vision?" I feel my mouth slacken. I don't mean to sound doubtful, but I never had Garrett down as the superstitious type.

"Yeah, like in my sleep."

"You mean a dream," I correct him.

"Call it what you want, I just saw it, and when I did, I realized it was what I wanted most in the whole world."

"You gonna tell me about it?" Now I'm intrigued.

"I was working in the yard on a warm, spring morning, and I looked up, and there ya were, standing right in that doorway," he redirects his eyes to the loft door in front of us. "You were standing beside your easel with a big, swollen belly, and ya had the brightest smile on your face when ya looked down at me. It was the most beautiful thing I ever saw." He looks down to where his palm is sliding across my flat stomach with a smile of his own.

"And then you got to work?" I reach up and twist a strand of his dark hair around my finger, wishing we hadn't wasted those three years apart.

"I used to watch this film with my grandpa about a guy who built this baseball field in his cornfield."

"Field of Dreams," I remember it well. One of Mom's ex-husbands was a huge baseball fan. It was his favorite film.

"That's the one. You remember that line from it? Build it, and they will come." I love the way he blushes a little; it's not often you catch Garrett embarrassed.

"I remember." I struggle to hide the huge smile I wanna make.

"Well, I kinda put all my faith into that."

"I love you," I tell him, feeling the urge to cry when all the happiness inside me reaches my eyes.

"And I never want ya to think I take that for granted." He kisses the back of my hand.

"I've expected a lot from you since you've been back, way more than I deserve. I've set the pace and barely let you breathe, and I'm sorry if sometimes I scare ya, but I've never wanted something the way I do you, and I will not let ya slip through my fingers again." When he moves in to kiss me, I suddenly remember a detail from his vision and quickly press my hand on his chest to hold him back.

"In this vision of yours, when you said I was big, how big are we talking?" I pout while I wait for his answer.

"Oh, you were pretty huge," his eyes stretch wide, "But ya looked hot as hell." I make a lame attempt to shove him away, but he snatches my wrist and shifts our bodies, so I'm laying back on the couch with him hovering over me.

He looks hungry as he looks down at me, and before he devours me completely, there's something I need him to know.

"I like the idea of carrying something of yours inside me." Sitting on my elbows, I make sure my lips brush against his jawline. "You don't scare me, Garrett Carson," I whisper.

It's been a whole month since Aubrey died, and my brother is still as angry as he was the day it happened. He's moved back home and now spends all his hours in the day working on the ranch and all the ones in the evening drinking.

Joe Mason is miraculously still breathing, but that's only because there's been no opportunity. Cole made a scene at the funeral and practically told the whole town that he was gonna kill Joe Mason, and with Swann still sniffing around town, we can't give her a third murder victim to add to her tally, not now that she'd know exactly who to come for if anything happened to Joe. All that is becoming irrelevant to Cole, though, he's like a grenade with the pin pulled. He could go up any second.

"Morning," Maisie breezes cheerfully into the dining room and breaks the silence, and Cole nods his head politely to her, getting back to eating his eggs.

"Morning darlin'," I nod, too, resisting the urge to drag her onto my lap and have her eat her breakfast from there. It seems insensitive to be that way with her while Cole suffers. I've been refraining and keeping my hands to myself when he's around, but it's difficult when you got a wife as hot as mine. She sits at the table wearing one of my tees over the cute pj shorts she loves, and there's a huge smile on her lips before she bites into the apple in her hand.

"You don't want anything cooked? I'm sure Josie would make you fresh eggs." I suggest.

"Not this morning," she shakes her head and keeps the adorable grin set on her face.

"You feeling ok?" I check, knowing damn well that there's something going on. Breakfast is, without a doubt, Maisie's favorite meal of the day.

"Not at all. I'm feeling great."

"Good," I nod back and smile at her.

"In fact, I'm real excited. Leia's picking me up in an hour, and we're heading to that Wedding Fayre she was meant to go to with Caleb," she points out, and it makes the smile drop right off my lips.

"Ain't that somethin' the groom should be doin' with her?" Wade steps in, heading straight for the table of food and slapping a huge spoonful of eggs on his plate. After loading on a few sausages, too, he places his plate on the space laid out next to Maisie, and the way she turns her nose up when she looks at his plate only confirms my suspicions.

"Well, today it's a matron of honor's job."

Wade tries his best not to look like he cares as he sticks his fork into his sausage and bites off the end. I'da thought seeing Cole lose Aubrey would have had him acting on the whole Leia situation, but it seems to have pulled him in the opposite direction. It doesn't make sense, and I'm starting to believe he's actually gonna let the girl go through with this marriage.

"I'll have Otis drive ya."

Maisie spins her head at me, and if looks could kill, I'd be flat out on the floor.

"I don't need to be escorted," she tells me. That pretty smile she was wearing a few seconds ago has suddenly turned venomous.

"I disagree, which is why Otis is coming with ya," I inform

her, hoping she ain't about to cause a scene in front of my brothers; she's been getting progressively pissed off at the fact I've had Otis watching over her whenever I can't be around. But since the night some fucker came into my home and went through my sister's things, I'm not taking any chances.

Instead of arguing back at me like I expect her to, she stands up from the table and tries her best to hold in her tears as she marches out the room.

I get up to follow her, and when Wade starts to laugh, I slap him hard across the back of his head as I pass him.

I rush up the stairs and find Maisie on the bed sobbing.

"Darlin, don't cry," I sound like I'm begging because I am. I hate seeing her upset, and worst of all, I don't know how to handle it. "I'm just tryin' to keep ya safe."

"It's suffocating, Garrett. What if me and Leia want to have a private conversation? I get that you want to keep me safe, and I love you for it but don't you think you're being a bit overbearing?" When she looks up at me and snuffles back her tears, I move cautiously and sit on the mattress beside her.

"You know you've been here almost two months, and ya ain't had a period yet," I point out, wondering if there's something else causing this reaction. I've done some research into the early signs of pregnancy since I've been trying to get her knocked up, and I think we can safely tick emotional outbursts off the checklist.

She lets out a heavy sigh and gets up, moving away from me and looking out the window.

"You shouldn't get your hopes up!" she snaps, refusing to make eye contact with me.

"Why not, it's what we want, ain't it?" I go to her, wrapping my arms around her waist and refusing to let her blank me out.

"Yes, it's what we want." There's a tiny hint of her smile when she eventually looks up at me.

"Okay, so at the risk of gettin' my face slapped here, d'ya think ya might be overreacting a little?" I point out.

"I don't think you are one to judge on overreacting," she looks up at me with a blank expression.

"Okay, ya got me on that. But until the person who killed your mom is locked up, I'm gonna overreact, and I'm gonna be overbearing."

"Garrett, we both have to face the fact that that may never happen. The police have nothing. So, what's your plan? To wrap me up in cotton wool for the rest of my life?"

"Whatever it takes," I try making light of the fact that's exactly what I plan to do, but she ain't budging on this.

"We have to face up to the fact we may never know who killed my mom."

She looks a little sad, and in a weird way, it brings me some relief. She's been so numb to the death of her mother that I've been worried about her.

"I'll find out," I promise, sliding my hand up her cheek and pulling her head up so her lips meet mine. She tastes like the apple she bit into downstairs, and it makes me want to taste more of her.

"Garrett," she pushes me with a very serious look on her face, "I'm gonna throw up." She gags a little before rushing toward the bathroom. I follow her, resting my shoulder against the door frame and watching her hurl into the toilet.

"Wipe that smug smile off your face, Garrett Carson!" She calls out, without even turning around, and when she reaches up to grab some tissues and turns back around to look at me, I let that smug smile she accused me of grow even bigger.

"You gonna let me get my hopes up now?" I ask.

CHAPTER 29

MAISIE

"So, are you gonna take a test?" Leia sounds excited as we walk back toward the car, where Otis is waiting for us.

"Will you keep your voice down. I told you it was a secret," I tell her, hoping that Otis is far enough away not to have heard. I shouldn't have told Leia, but she is my best friend, and I figure it's a pretty huge thing to keep myself.

"So, are you?" she asks again.

"Yes, Garrett said he'd pick one up today, and we can take it together tonight."

"And you will call me the second you know for sure?" The looks she's giving me dares me not to.

"Of course, I will."

"You do realize you are gonna be the size of a whale on my wedding day? At least I know there's no chance of you upstaging me." She bumps me with her hip.

"Leia, with the deposit you just put down on that makeup artist, I can assure you noone is going to upstage you." We both giggle as Otis opens the door for us to get in the back.

———

We're much later than we thought we'd be, and it's got dark real quick. We're still about half an hour from home, and as excited as I am about taking the test when I get there, I can't help feeling a little nervous. I've been seeing the signs for about a week, but the past few days they seem to have hit me with force. I'm queasy in the mornings, I'm tired all the time, and as much as I hate to admit it, Garrett was right about my outburst this morning. I know he only worries about me, and after what happened to his sister, I don't blame him for wanting to protect me. I guess if the test is positive, I'm gonna have to prepare for him to get a lot worse.

"So, are you bored of being Maisie's personal bodyguard yet?" Leia leans through the middle seat to ask Otis.

Otis is friendly enough and never acts as if watching me is a burden. I figure Garrett must trust him over a lot of the other bunkhouse guys to give him the job as my minder. That, and the fact he's built like a mountain.

"Not at all." He glances up into his rearview mirror and smiles.

"Still, bet you'd rather be chasing cattle around. Ain't that what cowboys are supposed to do?"

"A Copper Ridge cowboy does whatever's required," he points out, reminding me of the brand Garrett has on his chest. I wonder if Otis has one, too.

"Look at that fool." He shakes his head when a Dodge races to overtake us. There're headlights coming from the other side of the road, and it only just manages to make it through the gap. It makes me think of Aubrey and the night her friend died. I don't know if I'm allowed to share the information with Leia. I should, considering she's about to marry into that family, but she seems to have her mind set, and the last thing I wanna do is push her away. If the truth doesn't come out soon, though, I'm gonna have to intervene.

My cell starts to ring, and when I see Garrett's name flashing, I feel a dopey smile pull at my lips as I answer.

"Hello?"

"Hey, darlin'." I can tell straight away that something's wrong, there's an edge in his tone that he's trying to calm. "Where ya at?"

"We're about twenty minutes from home," I assure him, knowing how eager he is to do that test.

"Good, but I hate to say it. I ain't gonna be here when ya get back. I've had to deal with somethin'." He sounds more sad than angry, and I can't help feeling a little disappointed.

"Is everything ok?" I start to worry, whatever it is must be serious. Garrett hates being away from the ranch these days.

"Yeah, everythin's fine, and I won't be long. Just tell Otis to stick around until I get back. I don't want ya in the house all by..." I only just catch what he says before my cell cuts.

"Garrett?"

"That'll be the reception. Ya don't get shit around here; you'll get something back when we get over the hill," Otis assures me, flicking his eyes up into the mirror again.

"It's fine, I managed to get what he said, and I'm sorry to tell you, but you're stuck with me a little longer. Garrett had to take care of something."

"Not a problem, ain't too often I get the company of a beautiful woman, and although Garrett would have my eyeballs for it, he ain't around to catch me appreciating it." Otis winks, making me and Leia both laugh at him.

"See, didn't get ya nowhere, did it, jerk!" He calls out when he sees the Dodge that flew past us parked on the side of the road ahead with the hood up.

"They look like they're having car trouble." I glance back through the rear window. It's started to rain heavily since we've been on the road, and the vision's blurry through the glass, but I can just about make out a figure looking inside the hood.

"Well, the son of a bitch can call a tow truck. That, right there, is karma." Otis sniggers.

"Otis, you have to stop and help him, there could be kids in that car, and you just said yourself there isn't any cell phone reception."

Putting on the brakes and pulling over, he spins around in his seat to look at me.

"Are you determined to get me into heaven?" he asks.

"It's the decent thing to do, and you know it. We can call it your good deed for the day."

"I think I already did my good deed of the day when I pretended to be Miss Walker here's groom so she could enter that honeymoon competition." He looks at Leia, and she blushes when she recalls him carrying her through the inflatable obstacle course that one of the entertainment companies had set up.

"Which we would have won if you'd have let me hold you the way I wanted to. Over the shoulder never fails."

"All the blood was going to my head!" Leia defends herself.

"You two just stay here. I'll go see what the trouble is." Otis lets out a sigh before he gets out of the truck and slams the door.

"I gotta agree with him, you'd have had it in the bag if you hadn't insisted on him carrying you the way all the other couples were doing it." I shrug, and Leia shakes her head before taking out her cell and moving it around to try and get some reception.

We both jump when we hear the loud bang, and when we look back out the rear window, it's hard to see through the headlights glaring at us, but I swear Otis is on the floor.

"Fuck!" Leia gasps when the tall figure standing over him with a gun fires another bullet straight into him. His attention suddenly draws to the car, and when he starts walking toward us, I feel fear creep up my throat.

"We have to get out of here." Leia starts to climb into the driver's seat while I remain static. Too scared to move and too shocked to scream.

"*Come on!*" Leia frantically tries to start the engine, but her fingers just fumble the keys. I close my eyes and take back every word I ever said about Garrett being overprotective and wish he was here now.

Another loud shot goes off, making me scream and cover my ears, but it doesn't block out the sound of another one firing.

"He's shot out the tires." Leia looks out through the rear-view mirror in horror.

"What do we do?" I have to remind myself to breathe despite the fact my chest feels as though it's made of concrete.

"Run. If we head off the road, he'll be shooting into the dark. Come on." She climbs across the seat to the passenger side and opens the door to climb out.

"I don't wanna get shot at," I call out to her, but when my door handle starts to rattle, I realize I have no choice. I crawl across the backseat to the other side and open the door, jumping onto the grass verge and running into the open field. I glance around me to look for Leia, but I can't see any sign of her, and despite having no idea where I'm heading, fear keeps me running.

The gun goes off again, and when I feel no pain, I pray for Leia.

The ground under my feet is rough, and I stumble as I run into the open darkness, having no idea where I'm heading or if I'm gonna make it there.

The squelching of footsteps that comes from behind me tells me whoever this is, is close behind. I can't let panic take over, especially if he catches me. I'll have to fight, even if it hurts.

"Get back here!" the voice yells at me, and although I've

only covered a little ground, I can feel myself getting out of breath. My legs feel weak, my heart thumps like it's about to explode, and when I feel a huge shove come from behind me, I tumble to the ground.

My body gets turned over, so I'm lying on my back, and when a hand grips around my throat, it slams my head back hard into the ground. The heavy weight on top of me crushes, and I struggle against it with all the energy I have left. It's nothing in comparison to his strength. His strong hand stops choking me so he can pin me to the cold, wet dirt by my wrists and spit in my face. I decide I need to see who this man, who's intent on hurting me, is and when I look up, I can just make out a face I recognize in the light that the moon provides.

"Told ya I'd be seein' ya." Seth, the man I saw at Leia's party with old man Mason, sniggers as I struggle against his hold.

"Get off me!" I kick my legs, but it all seems so pointless.

"You ain't goin' nowhere." He releases one of my arms so he can push his hand between us, and when I hear his belt start to clink, I scream so loud I swear I'll wake the dead.

"Shut up!" He backhands my face, making my brain rattle. And when his palm covers over my mouth and nostrils, keeping my body pinned and suffocating me at the same time, I feel him start to lift up the dress I'm wearing. I taste the dirt from his fingers as I scream against them. I feel his breath on my skin, and it makes me want to vomit.

"Ya know what your boyfriend did to me, precious?" he asks with the full pressure of his heavy body on top of me and his cock pressing hard against my panties as he forces me to listen.

"He beat me bloody and tied me to a tree. He humiliated me in front of all those bunkhouse boys who hang on his every word and left me for dead. And all because his stupid, little bitch went wanderin' into the woods all alone." I try to raise my knee so I can hit him where it'll hurt, but he's got me held too tight.

"Now I'm gonna show Carson what happens to people who fuck with me. I'm gonna fuck ya cunt raw and slice you open. Then leave you for the wolves to tear apart." He spits at my face again while the hand that isn't covering my mouth rips at my panties. I feel his cock land on my skin, his wet, cold fist shaking it hard as he tries to locate my entrance, and I close my eyes and pray for a miracle.

I don't know if the loud moan I hear comes out of him or me, but when Seth's eyes turn vacant, and the whole weight of his body flops onto mine, I see Leia standing over him, holding something big and metal in her hand.

"Daddy's always telling me I should learn to use a car jack." She drops it to the floor and rests her hands on her knees, trying to catch her breath. "You have no idea how heavy that thing was to run with."

I use the last of my strength to struggle out from under his body.

"Come on." Leia straightens herself back up and grabs my hand.

"I'll bet I've only knocked him out, and I've watched enough scary movies to know that he's gonna be back on his feet chasing us any minute. We need to get back on the road."

Clasping my hand tight, she drags me into a jog, and I have to ignore the fact that every single muscle in my body is aching as we head back toward the car.

I keep checking over my shoulder for any sign of him chasing us, and when we eventually get to the road, and there's no sign of him behind us, I figure we've gained enough ground for me to catch my breath.

"Oh my god." I sink onto my knees when I see Otis lying on the ground with a bullet between his eyes.

"What we gonna do?" I look up at Leia helplessly, wondering how on earth she's being so strong.

"Well, we sure ain't gonna die." She drags me back up and leads me toward the Dodge.

I jump in the passenger seat and breathe a sigh of relief when Leia starts the engine and pulls onto the road. Now that the panic's over, I can feel a thumping in the back of my head, and when I reach around to try and rub it away, my hands become sticky. I don't recall hitting my head, but when I hold my fingers out in front of me, I see two hands instead of one and red, lots of red.

"Shit, Maisie, are you ok?" Leia's eyes flit between me and the road.

"Yeah, I just..." Everything around me turns blurry, darkening like I'm running through a narrowing tunnel until there's nothing but black and the sound of my friend screaming my name.

"Ya don't have to be here, you know," Cole reminds me and Wade as we sit beside him in the bar out in Columbus. The same bar I recall kicking Jason McIntyre's ass in for the first time.

"Course we do. We're your brothers." Wade reminds him, knocking back his beer.

He's right about that, besides we both know Cole's too hot-headed to be here by himself.

When he received a text from one of the ranch hands he used to work with at the Mason's, telling him he had information for him, I knew that whatever I had planned for me and Maisie tonight would have to wait. I get to hold my girl in my arms every night and know she's safe. Cole will never know what that feels like, and that's the reason I'm sitting right here beside him.

"There he is." He nods his head toward the door when a man walks through it. He's tall, broad, and got the kinda looks that have women on their knees, but I don't recall seeing him around town. Raising his hat, he takes a seat, and stares across the table at Cole nervously.

"Whatcha drinking, honey?" The waitress comes straight over, and he orders a beer before crossing his hands on the table.

"What ya got for me, Dexter?" Cole skips past all the pleasantries and gets straight to the point.

"I know what ya plannin'" Dexter speaks up, putting on a brave front.

"Trust me, your wildest imagination couldn't make it up." Cole calls his bluff and Dexter shifts uncomfortably in his seat.

"I know ya wanna kill Joe Mason." He leans forward and lowers his voice so those surrounding us don't hear.

"I don't *wanna* kill him. I'm *gonna* kill him." Cole leans forward, too, whispering darkly.

"Yeah, well, I'm here to tell ya that ya got him all wrong." Dexter looks shifty, his eyes keep peering at the door like he's expecting someone to come through it, and it has my guard up.

"Joe didn't kill Aubrey." He focuses on the beer that gets put in front of him.

"Laurie Cross was singing that same tune until I shot off his left nut," Cole points out, sitting back in his chair and crossing his arms over his chest confidently.

"Joe got Laurie to lie for him, because he couldn't say where he really was that night. Joe is innocent, he didn't kill either of those women, and I can swear to that because he was with me." Dexter stares at my brother across the table, his posture has suddenly changed, and the look in his eyes is dangerous, like a mother bear protecting her cub.

"There's a place we go, a motel, and he was there with me. The night ya pa's wife got shot and the morning Aubrey got killed."

I watch Cole's eyes widen as he takes in what Dexter's trying to tell him.

"Whoa, steady up. Are ya tellin' me that you and Joe Mason are...?"

"That's what I'm tellin' ya, and if he knew I was here, he'd string me up for it. But I know your reputation, ya ain't men who make threats without seein' 'em through, and I won't have him die just because his daddy thinks he's a sinner." Dexter picks up his beer and takes a long swig.

I'm as stunned as my brothers, but I'm starting to see how this might all fall together. Ronnie Mason always has been a narrow-minded ass. If what we're hearing is true, I can't imagine him being very open to his son's lifestyle choices. It makes me wonder if this is the reason Ronnie Mason was so intent on getting Aubrey to marry Joe.

"And ya sayin' you were with him when Aubrey died? This ain't some cover up because if it is, I'll do more than shoot off a testical."

"I can prove it. Soon as I found out about Aubrey, I called the motel and asked for a copy of their CCTV footage. It's clear enough for ya to see us gettin' out of the car and entering the room. It shows when we left, too. Joe just won't use it."

"Why?" Cole shakes his head, trying to make sense of it all.

"Because Joe's had to hide who he is his whole life. His father forced that poor girl to marry him, and every day he forces Joe to be someone he ain't."

"Aubrey told me her and Joe were lookin' to start a family." Cole is yet to be convinced.

"Because the old man was demanding' it. Joe can be an asshole out on the yard, but when it comes to his old man, he's got no backbone. Cole, everyone on that ranch knew ya loved Mrs. Mason. The whole damn town knew it."

"Don't ya fuckin' call her that!" Cole hisses through his teeth, slamming his fist hard at the table.

"I understand that, what I'm here askin' ya to believe, goes against everything you've been seein' for however many years you've been suffering, but I'm tellin' ya, it's the truth. Joe and Aubrey's marriage was a mask, one that Ronnie Mason needed them to wear because he's ashamed of the real man his son is."

I can tell by the passion Dexter speaks with that he's telling the truth, and for the first time in my life, I find myself feeling sorry for a Mason brother. Who in this world has the right to tell another being who they're allowed to love?

"I wanna talk to him myself." Cole stands up, looking overwhelmed by what's just been revealed.

"He won't do that; he'd never forgive me if he thought I was here. He's petrified of his father," he scowls, showing how much that rattles his cage.

"You tell him, from me, that he doesn't need to hide who he is from us. Ain't no judgment here. All I want is the fuckin' truth. I wanna know who killed my girl, and if he can look me in the eye and tell me ya story's true, then ya might have just saved that man's life." Cole stands up, letting us know that it's time for us to leave, and Wade finally picks up his cell, that's been vibrating like crazy, outta his pocket as we head out the door.

"Leia, Leia, calm the fuck down! I can't understand whatcha sayin'!," he shouts, blocking his other ear from all the background noise.

"What!" I don't like the shock in his tone or the way he looks at me as he listens to what she's saying.

"Okay, listen to me. Stay calm, we're comin' ok?" He hangs up and comes toward me, his expression wavering between fear and concern.

"Garrett, I need ya to give me the keys to the truck." He holds out his hand.

"What was that call about?" I ask, sensing something is very fucking wrong.

"Hand over the keys, and I'll tell ya." He steadies his breath and tries to stay calm, and I grab him by his shirt collar and slam him into the wall.

"Ya tell me right the fuck now what that call was about!" I warn.

"That was Leia, she's at the hospital." He closes his eyes, and I feel him swallow against the hand I've got his shirt gripped in.

"Where's Maisie?" Fear causes me to shake as I tighten my grip.

"She's there, too. She's the reason they're there. They were attacked on the road on their way home. Otis is dead," he tells me, and I drop him instantly, racing for the truck.

"Garrett, Wade's right, ya shouldn't drive." Cole tries to stand in my way, but I shove past him to get to the wheel.

"Garrett!" He comes back at me and shoves me against the truck. He presses his forearm against my throat while his other hand feels in my jacket for the keys.

"We're goin' straight there, but I'm drivin'" he tells me, slowly releasing me and getting behind the wheel. Instead of arguing, I rush around the other side and hop in the passenger seat, and Wade wastes no time getting in beside me.

Cole drives like a maniac to get us to the hospital, and when he screeches the tires to a halt outside the ER, I get out and rush inside.

"Garrett." Leia's standing in the corridor, covered in dirt, with a worried look on her face and her eyes swollen from crying.

"What happened?" I grab both her arms like I'm gonna shake the truth out of her, but all she does is cry.

"Tell me!" I yell, feeling a hand grip at my shoulder and tug me away.

"Get off her." Wade forces me back and tries to get some sense out of her while I look around for a doctor.

"Hey, you!" I block the path of a woman wearing a white coat.

"I'm looking for Maisie Carson. I mean Wildman. Hell, I don't know what name she's under, but she's got blonde hair and..."

"Calm down, sir." She speaks to me in a condescending tone that only gets me more frustrated.

"I can't calm down. I need to know where she is."

"And who are you, sir?" she asks.

"I'm her husband!" I snap, noticing from the corner of my eye that Wade and Leia have both fallen silent and are staring at me in shock.

"Husband?" Wade checks he's heard right.

"Your wife is in room four. Follow me." The doctor smiles and turns around, and I leave my brother and the woman he's in love with, gawking in shock, to follow her.

"Seth?" I check I'm hearing right as Leia explains what happened. She's shivering, and all I wanna do is wrap her up in my arms and hold her the way Garrett does when he's around Maisie.

"And did he?" Cole freezes from pacing the floor in front of the plastic chairs where we're sitting.

"No, I got there just in time, knocked him out with a car jack." She smiles a little, and I'm jealous of the tear that slides down her cheek and spills between her lips.

"You hit him with a car jack?" Cole laughs. It must be the first time I've seen him smile since Aubrey died, and it gives me a little hope that he ain't completely numb.

"I had to improvise, it was heavy as hell. I don't know how I carried it so far, but I wasn't about to let that asshole hurt her. It was too late for Otis." Her eyes lift back up to mine, filling with more sadness, and I pull her head down onto my shoulder, soothing my hand over her hair while I glance up at my brother. He nods his head. He knows what needs to be done, and before he leaves, he crouches down in front of us to talk to Leia.

"Where did it happen?" he asks, sounding oddly calm.

"On the road between The Pillington Junction and Fork River, we had to leave Otis on the road. Someone would have found him by now, and I don't know if I hit Seth hard enough for him to be dead. What if he comes after me?" She starts to panic again.

"Ain't gonna happen. Wade here's gonna take ya home, and I'm gonna figure out what happened to Seth and take care of it. He can't hurt ya now."

"I'm not leaving until I know Maisie's okay. They rushed her through those doors, and no one's telling me anything."

"Shhhh, don't worry. We can stay until we get an update," I assure her, watching my brother stand up straight and scratch his jaw.

"Call ya dad and let him know what happened, he's gonna wanna know you're safe." I grab hold of Cole and drag him out of earshot.

"If that fucker's still alive, Garrett's gonna want him brought in."

"I'll round up the boys and make it happen. We'll find him. You just take care of ya girl."

"She ain't my girl." I look across at her and draw in a breath my chest feels like it can't quite finish. She's safe, a little shook up. But it's gonna be ok. She's got her cell pressed to her ear and even covered in mud, with half her hair hanging out of its ponytail; she looks beautiful.

"We both know that ain't true, Wade." Cole grabs the top of my arm and smiles again before heading out of the glass doors to go in search of Seth.

"Hey," I quickly chase after him when a thought comes to my mind.

"What Dexter said back at the bar, if it's true..."

"If it's true, me and Aubrey ain't the only ones who've been suffering. The man who caused it will be the one who pays the price."

"I wish we could end him as easily as we can Seth." I feel for Cole, the Masons have been untouchable since Aubrey died, and I know he won't even begin to feel better until the person who killed her pays.

"That's if she hasn't ended Seth already." I notice him snigger as he looks over at Leia.

"If she did..."

"Don't worry, I got it covered, bro," he promises, making his way toward the truck and already pressing his cell to his ear to call in some help.

"So, Maisie and Garrett are married." I hear her voice, and when I turn around, Leia's standing right behind me. She's trying to be brave, but I can tell by the quivering of her lips that she's still scared.

"Yeah, first I heard of it, too, but it ain't a surprise. Garrett's one of those guys. Once he knows what he wants, he'll stop at nothin' to get it."

"And what about you, do you know what you want from this crazy world?" She sighs, looking up into my eyes like maybe she can read the thoughts behind them.

"You wouldn't believe me if I told ya." I tuck the hair that's fallen on her face behind her ear and let my hand linger there a little longer than it should.

"Try me." Her lips ain't trembling anymore, they're smiling, and I wonder if this could be the moment. The one where I tell her I've wanted her my whole life.

"I..."

"Leia!" The voice breaks our eye contact, and when I look to the doors and see Caleb rush through them, I feel the chain snap back around my chest as I swallow down my words.

"Thank God you're okay." He snatches Leia in his arms and kisses the top of her head, peering at me over the top of it with cold eyes that I want to force into the back of his skull.

"I'm fine, honestly. It's Maisie that's hurt." She gently eases him away and smiles at me awkwardly.

"Well, I'm here now. I can take you home." Caleb takes her

hand, and I notice how his knuckles turn white when she tries to pull away.

"Don't make a scene," he whispers in her ear, tugging her closer and holding her firm.

"I just want to check Maisie's alright." She manages to get her arm free and looks determined as she stares back at him.

"Look, you don't wanna spend all night here. My father knows the hospital administrator, he'll arrange for you to get updates. Come on."

"I don't want updates; I want to see my friend," Leia argues back, and I have to hide the smirk I'm trying not to make under my hand.

"Fine, we'll wait here!" Mason snarls at me as he places his armsaround her shoulders and leads her to sit back down. I don't go with them. I stand on the other side of the room with my shoulders pressed against the wall, watching the way he keeps her tucked in the crook of his arm and wishing I was him.

I sit by her bed, waiting for her to wake up, with my toes tapping against the floor and my hands linked together because I have no idea what to do with 'em. The doctors tell me she's fine, but I won't believe it until I see her awake for myself. Her face is bruised, one of her eyes is swollen, and her lip is split. I swear, when I find out who's responsible for this, I won't just kill him, I'll make sure he suffers all the way to hell and bleeds out at the gates.

She stirs, but not in a good way. Like she's haunted by something and reliving it, and all I can do is reach out and hold her hand in mine.

"Garrett?" I lift my head up when I hear her voice and watch her eyes blink as they adjust to the light.

"Maisie." I stand up and take her face in my hand, forcing her to look at me and focus, "Are ya okay?" My heart is beating outta control while I wait for her to say something else.

"I think so. My head really hurts." She raises the hand, I'm not gripping, up to her head and touches the bandage that's wrapped around it.

"Doc said ya took a hit to it, but you're gonna be ok," I assure her, resisting the urge to wrap her up in my arms in case I hurt her.

"What happened?" I ask, trying my best to keep my calm.

Leia told Wade on the phone that they'd been attacked, but that's all I know.

"It was Seth, that guy you sacked from the ranch." She looks away from me and covers her face with her hand.

"Look at me, tell me what happened." I steady my breathing, fully aware that I can't be losing my shit right now.

"He killed Otis, then he chased after me, and I thought he was gonna...." Her eyes squeeze closed, and she swallows heavily. "I could feel him right there, and then Leia saved me." She breaks down, and I gently cradle her delicate face in my hands and make sure those blue eyes look into mine.

"Ya safe now. He can't hurt ya," I promise, trying not to let the rage inside me tense in my fingers and crush her.

"I don't know if he's dead or alive, he didn't chase after us... but,"

"Shhh, ya don't need to worry about that. Ya need to focus on gettin' better," I whisper, trying to keep her as calm as I can.

"Did you mention the baby to the doctors? What if...?"

"I told them that we suspected but weren't sure, and they wanted to let ya rest a little. Said they'd send someone down when ya woke up."

"What if something's happened?" She bites her lips as a fresh batch of tears brim in her eyes, and it makes me want to destroy anyone who Seth fucking Granger ever cared about.

"We didn't know for sure darlin'..." I try to reassure her.

"*I* knew. I could sense it, and I don't think I sense it anymore." I can see her starting to panic, and I have no idea how I'm supposed to calm her down while I'm hanging on the edge of destruction myself.

"Sweetheart, you're probably feelin' a lot of things that would override that right now." I try to stop my hand from shaking as I brush it over her cheek and wipe away her tears.

"I need to know Garrett, please!" she begs, and since there

ain't a single thing in this world I wouldn't do for her, I kiss her forehead and head out the door to find a doctor.

———

It's a long wait until we hear a gentle knock at the door, and a woman wheeling a computer, on a trolley, lets herself in.

"Maisie, I'm a sonographer. Dr. Harper tells me you suspect you might be pregnant?" I stand and observe as Maisie nods her head nervously.

"I can take a look and see what's happening."

"Yes, please." Maisie reaches out her hand for mine, squeezing it tight and taking a steady breath.

"When was your last period?" the woman asks, resting on the edge of the bed and pulling on some gloves.

"I don't really keep track."

"She's been in Fork River for nine weeks and two days, and she's not had one," I answer for her, earning myself a shocked look from them both.

"Ok, I'm gonna use this probe to do an internal examination. Is that okay?" she checks, and Maisie nods her head enthusiastically, sliding down the bed a little further and opening her knees under the covers to give the nurse access.

I watch as she looks up at the ceiling and closes her eyes like she's saying a little prayer, and when I realize that she wants this just as much as I do, it makes me even more nervous.

She keeps her eyes closed, and I kiss the top of her head and squeeze her hand tighter while we wait.

"Have you had any symptoms?" the sonographer asks curiously.

"Some, I've felt sick. I was sick this morning, and I'm a little on the emotional side." Maisie blushes a little when she looks up at me, and I can tell from the way she's trying not to cry that, whether the time is now or later, Maisie Carson is gonna make the most amazing mother.

"And have you had any fertility treatment?" I notice the curious look that suddenly falls on the woman's face.

"No, we hadn't taken a test yet, but I would have seen a doctor right after," Maisie assures her, as her blue eyes glisten with more worry.

"I was referring to fertility drugs or IVF; it's given to couples who are struggling to conceive naturally."

"Oh, well, we only just started trying. Do you think I need it?" Now she's really looking worried, and I wish there was something I could say to make her relax.

"Certainly not. I think what we're looking at here is your own tiny miracle." The sonographer smiles and turns the screen to face us.

"You see these?" She points to a tiny cluster of bean-shaped shadows. "All three of those have good strong heartbeats."

"Three?" I lean in closer and study the screen.

"Yes, triplets are rarely conceived naturally, that's why I asked about fertility treatments. Right now, these are measuring at around seven weeks."

"And they're all ok?" Maisie asks, looking shocked as she stares at the three dots on the screen herself.

"All look healthy. I will warn you that a triplet pregnancy is considered high risk, and we'll want to keep a closer eye on you than we do some of the other mothers in our care, but for now, you can rest assured that your babies are fine."

"Holy shit!" I blow out a breath and fall into the seat behind me.

"I'll leave you to get over the shock and arrange for your nurse to schedule a follow-up appointment with a doctor who specializes in multiples." She rips off a printout from the machine and hands it to Maisie, who stares at the picture, mesmerized, while the woman wheels out the trolley and leaves us.

"Ya scared now?" I sit on the bed beside her and wrap my arm around her shoulder, staring at the image in her hand and wondering how the hell I ever got this lucky.

"Three!" She looks up at me. "Three babies, all at once."

"Well, we *did* work pretty hard at it." My comment earns me an elbow to the stomach, but I don't care. I can't remember a time when I've ever been happier.

"How are we gonna cope with this? A few weeks ago I was in L.A hating your ass and now we're..."

"Having three babies together, Mrs. Carson." I kiss her lips before she can try and convince me that this is anything other than perfect.

"Can we come in?" The door creaks open, and Leia pokes her head around it.

"Sure," Maisie calls her inside, and when she's followed closely by my brother, he's got a tense look on his face.

"You good?" Wade heads straight for Maisie and kisses her cheek. I can tell from the relief on his face when she nods, that he's been worried about her, too.

"And what about the...?" Leia gives Maisie a look that confirms she already told her she thought she was pregnant.

"Had it confirmed." Maisie nods her head, and her excited smile shows she's got no doubts. She knows we got this.

"And everything's ok?" Leia checks.

"They're all fine." Maisie hands over the picture, and Leia must notice the three little beans because she squeals so loud it hurts my ears.

"Does someone wanna clue me in as to what the fuck's goin' down here?" Wade stares at the girls blankly.

"You're gonna be an uncle," I tell him, watching his eyes flick between me and Maisie and a smile pulling on his lips.

"Three times over." Leia hands him the sonogram photo, and he looks up at me and shakes his head in amazement.

"Ya gotta be kiddin' me?"

I shrug my shoulders and watch Wade hug Maisie tight before he reaches over the bed to pull me in for one, too.

"Leia, keep your eye on her, she hasn't had anything to eat since she woke up. I'm gonna go grab her somethin'." I nod my head toward the door, so my brother knows to follow me, and leading him toward the vending machine, I keep my voice low.

"Seth Granger." I force the name out of my mouth, hating that I have to think about him at a time like this.

"Already got it covered. Cole's lookin' for him as we speak. He called a few minutes ago, only one body was found at the scene; that was Otis." We both look at the ground when we think about the fact Otis is gone. He was a good man, and I'm taking the fact he's dead as a sign that he did whatever he could to protect the girls we care about.

"When he's found, have Cole take him to the line camp. Put a bag over the fucker's head and tie him up. I want him under 24-hour supervision until I can get to him. Right now, Maisie's my priority."

"Ya thinkin' he might have been the one who killed Aubrey? 'Cause if he is, Cole ain't gonna wait for ya," Wade warns.

"He was with Cole and the others the morning she died, it can't have been him, but that don't mean he didn't kill Cora. We'll get our answers," I assure him, selecting Maisie's favorite candy bar before heading back to her room.

"Hey, congratulations on the weddin'," Wade tells me before I open the door.

"I'm sorry I couldn't tell ya, Maisie didn't think it was appropriate with what happened to Aubrey, and she didn't want to ruin Leia's big day." I watch the smile on my brother's face fade when I remind him of that.

"Yeah, well, I'm happy for ya. Real happy." He slaps my back and then grips my shirt before I move on.

"Just for reference. I woulda been the best man had ya done it all proper, right?"

"Sure," I nod before hurrying to get back to my wife.

CHAPTER 33

MAISIE

"**W**hatcha doin'?" Garrett startles me when he steps into his office.

"Just some research." I try smiling my way out of trouble, but the stern frown he stares back at me proves I'm unsuccessful.

"Doctors said ya should be takin' it easy; you've been home for less than five hours." He steps around his desk to see what I'm looking at, and I rest back in the chair and wait for him to scold me.

"Maisie, ya got enough shit to worry about without playin' detective." He sighs when he realizes I'm going through the files that were hacked from Investigator Swann's computer.

"This is keeping me out of trouble." I stare up at him innocently.

"I doubt that." He doesn't look convinced.

"Don't get mad, just let me get on with it," I beg. I've been going crazy since the attack, my head is trying to put everything together, and nothing makes sense.

"I'm not mad," Garrett tells me softly.

"Good, because I'm pretty sure you're not entitled to get mad with the woman who's growing three of your babies." I smile and place a hand on my stomach just to remind him.

"You will be the death of me." He rolls his eyes. "So d'ya have anything?" He focuses back on the screen.

"I have everyone who it can't be." I sigh, feeling deflated.

"And anything that links your mom to Aubrey?" he checks. I haven't seen Cole since I got discharged from hospital, but Garrett told me all about the meeting they had with Dexter. And now we're back to square one, with no idea who killed my mom or if the two murders are related.

"I'm more than certain old man Mason's behind it all," Garrett says his thoughts out loud, and I know that having no evidence to back that up is bothering him.

"He wouldn't have done the job himself, so the police ain't ever gonna pin it to him."

"So, what, he's just gonna get away with it?" I question, becoming more and more frustrated.

"No, there's no chance of that. Cole's got a mark on his head, but he can't strike too soon."

"And what about Seth? Have you got a mark on his head?" I shudder when I think about him, I can't close my eyes without seeing his face, and as hard as I try to keep that from Garrett, I know he can sense it. He's trying so hard not to be angry when he's around me, but I know all the tension inside him is gonna have to release some time.

"Nelson told ya; they got him custody," he assures me, avoiding eye contact and quickly changing the subject.

"Ya should stop lookin' at this shit and focus on something positive. Ya got three babies to shop for, so why dontcha call Leia and have her come over to online shop?"

"If you hurt him, I wanna see it." I place my hand on Garrett's arm. I don't know how, but I know there will come a time when Garrett makes Seth pay for what he did, and after what that man put me through and the things he could have cost me, I want to watch him suffer.

"No, you don't." Garrett shakes his head at me and clenches his jaw.

"I do. When I was in that field with him on top of me, I thought I was gonna die. I wanna see that fear in *his* eyes."

"Maisie, I'm not just gonna hurt him, I'm gonna kill him. And if ya watch that happen, you're gonna see a side to me that I'd rather ya didn't."

"You don't scare me," I remind him.

"Your husband, the man ya lookin' at right now, who's gonna love our kids with all his heart and kisses ya goodnight before he tucks ya up in his arms, *he* don't scare you. But the man I become when I step out that door and have to protect all those things I care about..." He flares his nostrils, "... sometimes *I'm* even scared of him," he warns, looking ashamed.

Standing up, I slide my palm over his cheek and drag his eyes back to mine.

"I never want you to hide from me," I tell him, hoping that he has enough faith in me to believe I can handle it.

"I'm tryin' to find the balance, Maisie, and the only way I can do it is to keep ya separate from it. Please give me that." I back down and nod, trying to hide my disappointment.

"I've upset ya, and I didn't wanna do that. I want ya to..."

"You didn't upset me, you're protecting me, and that's a great idea about Leia." I smile at him before I get up from his desk to go call her.

"Wait up." He comes after me, grabbing my hand and spinning me around and when I look up at him and wait for what he's got to say, he seems all out of words.

"I love ya," he tells me, before he kisses me, and I get the impression he just backed out of telling me something when he smiles sadly and heads out the door.

I go upstairs, and instead of going to our room to take my cell off charge and call Leia, I head toward the room my mom shared with Bill. Her expensive perfume still lingers in the air, and when I lie on the bed and look at the wedding photo on the nightstand, I wonder if there was a time in her life when she was ever happy.

I can't remember a smile of hers that wasn't fake, or a laugh she made at something genuine.

My eyes fill with tears when I think about that, and I don't know if it's the pregnancy hormones that put a pain in my chest like it's being scraped out, but I hate that it's there. My mom never knew love because she was always seeking something better. Something more than the man she was with and something more than me. I touch my hand to my stomach again and promise that my babies will always be enough.

"I'm sorry you're dead." I speak to her picture as my tears drop onto her pillow. "I'm sorry that you'll never know how it feels to be truly happy, but I don't think I can ever forgive you." I close my eyes so I don't have to look at it anymore, and for the first time since I learned that she'd died, I cry for her.

"Darlin'." I hear Garrett's voice as he stirs me from my sleep and realize I must have dropped off.

"Whatcha doin? in here?" he asks, kissing my cheek.

"I was just feeling a little sorry for her," I confess, looking back at the picture of our parents.

"Ya wanna talk about it?" He takes my hand in his.

"No, there's nothing to talk about. She's irrelevant now."

"Ya ever wonder what they might have been like as grandparents?" Garrett laughs, and he gets this beautiful smile on his face whenever he talks about the babies, one that makes my heart flutter and forget how overwhelming it all is.

"Disastrous!" I laugh, too, when I imagine my mother dealing with three crazy toddlers. "You wondering how we're gonna pull this off?" I ask him seriously.

"I'm pretty sure we ain't gonna sleep for like eight years, and I'm certain I'm gonna turn gray overnight, but if you're okay with that, I think we're gonna be just fine."

"I think I'd like a silver fox." I roll on top of him and tease his lips with mine, and when he grabs the back of my head and forces my lips harder onto his, sliding his other one into the front of my jeans, I quickly pull away.

"God, I'm sorry I wasn't thinkin'. Are ya okay with this?" He looks panicked, and when I realize he thinks I've stopped him because of what happened the other night, I quickly shake my head.

"No, I want you to, I *need* you to, but we can't do it here." I look around the room to remind him of where we are, and a wicked smile pulls on his lips.

"Maisie Carson, you're my wife, and I can fuck ya in any room I want to." He pulls my head back down onto his lips again, and reaches across to the photo on the nightstand, slamming it face down before he gets back to making me feel whole again.

"No, get off!" Her feet kick out, and when I reach out to touch her, she's soaking wet. "Stop, please," she begs, and I shake her to try and wake her up. We've been home three nights, and she's had one of these night terrors every night since.

"Darlin', wake up." I shake her a little harder, trying to pull her out of her hell, but she keeps her eyes shut tight, and when she clutches at my arm and screams, I feel like I'm gonna explode from all the anger I've been keeping inside me. I haven't left her side since all this happened. I haven't unleashed all the fucking fury I've been building up for Seth, and know I can't keep it in any longer.

"Maisie!" I shout her name. Her eyes shoot open, and when she sees me, she clings to me like the world is spinning and I'm her anchor.

"He had me pinned to the ground," she tells me breathlessly, and the sick taste in my throat makes me gag. I can't allow myself to envision it; if I do, I'll never come back from it.

"I got ya," I promise, holding her tight and trying to calm myself. Nothing is working, not when I know he's out at the line camp, sitting and waiting for me to put him through hell.

"What if he gets bail? And they won't put him away

forever; it could be his first offense. I figure we'll be lucky if he gets a year. If he killed my mom, there's no way to prove it." She can't get her words out fast enough, and all I can do is try to tell her it's gonna be ok.

"Go back to sleep," I lay down with her, stroking her hair and thinking about all the ways I can make Seth Granger suffer while I wait for her to stop shaking and drop back off again.

It's 3 am when I finally slide my arm from under her body and get up. Throwing on some clothes, I head across the hall to Wade's room to wake him.

"It's time." I pick up his boots and launch them at him, then fire out a text to Noah as I head out to the bunkhouse to wake up Tate, Finn, Dalton and Mitch.

"I need someone to stay here with her," I tell Mitch, thinking of Otis and the way he paid with his life to protect her. He wasn't a branded man, but he'll be remembered like one.

"Cole's at the line camp keeping watch, he hasn't left that fucker's side. You want me to stay with her? As much as I'd like to see him suffer, I think Wade will wanna see it more."

"Oh, I'll make sure you see him suffer. Go on over to the house, make yourself a coffee. I'll be in touch."

I nod to the others to follow me, and when they head for the trucks, I call 'em back.

"We ain't taking the trucks."

"What?" Dalton still looks half a fucking sleep.

"You're cowboys, ain't ya?" I redirect them to the stables and set to work saddling up Thunder.

It's four miles to the line camp cabin, and when we get there, Cole comes to the door and lights himself a cigarette.

"It's about time," he tells me.

"How did it go?" I ask, knowing that everyone's taken it in turns trying to get him to break and confess that he's been doing old man Mason's dirty work. I'm convinced he was the one who killed Cora.

"It ain't him. No one takes the rag and water for that long without squeakin'," Cole assures me.

"Okay," I nod, accepting my brother's decision. We can't keep him alive forever, and if he ain't got nothing to tell us, he ain't got a purpose.

"So, whatcha got planned?" he asks, and seeing the headlights in the distance coming our way, I smile and get ready to show him.

"Someone better be fucking dyin'." Sawyer leaves his headlights on as he gets out of the driver's seat and comes toward us. He's followed by Zayne and Noah, who both look equally as pissed off.

"Sorry to get you up so early."

"Early? We hadn't gone to bed yet." Zayne scratches the back of his head, while Noah listens for what I've got to say.

"Ya pick up what I needed?" I ask.

"Yeah," Sawyer smiles, as him and Zayne put on some gloves and head to the back of the truck to lift out the roll of barbed wire.

"Ya gotta to be kidding," Wade looks impressed as he watches them place it beside me.

"Well, don't just stand there. Bring out the guest of honor," I tell him.

I stand waiting, high on fucking adrenaline, knowing all that anger I've been holding onto is about to get its release.

Cole and Wade bring a beaten and bruised Seth Granger out of the cabin with his hands roped behind his back, and a dirty rag in his mouth to keep him silent.

Cole kicks the back of his legs so that he falls on his knees in front of me, and the first thing I do is shove my knee into his face.

"I should have ended ya that night myself, you're so fuckin' rancid even the wolves didn't want ya." Cole lifts him back up. This time, standing him up so we're eye to eye.

"What kinda man fights a war with another, by hurtin' a woman? You're about to feel what it's like to be helpless, to be scared and to have your life in the hands of someone else." I step back and take the brown gloves from my back pocket while all the others stand and spectate.

"That don't make you a man." I pull them over my hands and take the knife out of my belt.

His eyes flick left to right, bulging with fear when I press the point of it under his nose.

"You're gonna know what it's like to feel exposed and humiliated." I rip what's left of his shirt off his body and tear the blade through his underpants, watching the beads of sweat pour from his head when I hold the steel against his cock.

"You really think you were gonna fuck my wife with that thing?" I look down at it and snigger, acting like the thought doesn't make me wanna rip my heart out my chest to stop it from hurting.

"No wonder you gotta rape a girl to get that thing wet," I whisper, circling around him and watching the humiliation sink deeper and deeper into his head.

"I've had four days to think about how this could happen. *Four* days of rage and anger that I've kept all for you." I spit on his face and watch my saliva trickle down his cheek.

"When I was a boy, Mitch told me about something him and my uncle did to a man who stole some cattle once. I was so young I had nightmares about it. And I remember thinkin' that you'd really have to hate someone to wanna make 'em hurt like that."

I step back and pick up the barbed wire, and as I step toward him, he must figure out what's coming because he mumbles against the gag and makes a lame attempt to struggle out of Cole's hands.

I take my time, starting with his ankles and slowly wrapping it up his body. Listening to him muffle in agony as it pierces his skin and drags his flesh. Blood is already pouring from the incisions, and when I get all the way up to his shoulders, I stand back and admire my handy work.

Seth shakes his head, and I wish Maisie could see the tears of agony coming out of his eyes and the petrified look on his face.

I move over to Thunder and grab my rope, punching Seth hard in the face when I return and knocking him onto the floor. He screams through the gag as the sharp metal slices deeper into his skin, and I reach down to tie up his ankles, making sure the rope's secure before I pull the gag from his mouth.

"You better stay alive," I whisper before I stomp on his face and pick up the slack of the rope.

I jump on my saddle, tying my end of the rope to the front of it and look back at the others.

"Let's take this fucker for a ride," I tell them, squeezing my legs around Thunder's belly and clicking him on to head for the ranch.

Seth's screaming turns silent after the first mile, but I don't stop to check if he's still alive, I keep on riding. The others catch up quick, and the River Boys honk their horn. They slam their hands on the side of the truck, whooping like they're herding cattle, when they veer off from the follow party to get on the track that'll lead them to the road.

I ride as fast as Thunder can manage, hoping Seth feels every bump and ridge of Carson ground I drag him over.

I'm only a couple hundred yards away from the house, and I don't have to turn on my saddle to know the fucker's alive; I can hear him whimpering.

"What are you doing, Garrett?" Wade looks doubtful as he rides up beside me.

"She asked me if she could watch," I tell him, resting my elbow on the front of my saddle and trying to make a decision.

"Are you shittin' me?" He lowers his voice so the others can't hear.

"I thought the same thing you are, Wade. I was never gonna let her see it." I look at the ranch in front of me, the one I want Maisie to build all her hopes and dreams around, and my chest squeezes when I think about the pain he still puts her through.

"He haunts her, Wade." I pull on my rope to steady Thunder, it's been a long ride for him, dragging Seth's weight, and he's eager to get home.

"I get that, Garrett, but this...it's a lot." He looks back at Seth's shredded-up body, and he's right. It's hideous, probably beyond anything Maisie's ever had to see, and I caused it.

"Yeah, it's a lot, but she needs to know that she doesn't have to fear him anymore." The sun's coming up now, and sunrises at Copper Ridge are always beautiful. I got it all, right on the other side of that fence, and what stands this side could quite easily ruin it. But I made my wife a promise. No secrets, and so the choice will be hers, not mine.

I pull out my cell and call her. It takes her a while to answer, and when she does, she sounds so sleepy and sweet it almost makes me back out.

"Garrett, where are you? It's early."

"Yeah, darlin', it's early." I smile to myself when I envision her in our bed. "Listen, I had Sheriff Nelson tell you a lie the other day, and before you shout at me for it, I want ya to hear why,"

It surprises me that she remains silent and lets me explain.

"I knew Seth couldn't hurt you because the mornin' after he attacked you, Cole and the River Boys found him. I've had him held at the line camp ever since." I look at our bedroom window and wonder what face she's pulling right now.

"I got him right here." I swallow back my fear. "He's as good as dead, and I'm not gonna lie to ya, darlin', it ain't pretty."

"Garrett, where are you?" I can't make out if she's worried or mad, but knowing her, it's probably both.

"You asked me if you could watch, and I said no because I'm terrified that you'll never look at me with those big, blue, innocent eyes in the same way if you see what kinda man I can be."

"Garrett..."

"But, I'd rather risk that than have you suffer the fear this man put inside you," I interrupt her, before I lose my nerve.

"I'm not bringing this shit to our doorstep; bad shit only happens this side of the fence. So, if you're sure this is really what you want, and you need to stare into his face and watch him suffer his last breath, you have Mitch drive you out here to me. Okay, baby?"

I hang up when my voice goes weak, and clutching my fist, I wait.

"You sure about this?" Cole rides up to my other side.

"It's her choice." I swallow down the lump in my throat.

"We've let 'em take too much." I stare at everything around us that we fight for. I thought it meant a lot to me before, but now with three kids coming, I feel even more protective of it. I want them to have something, to be part of our family history. I want my brothers' kids to have it, too. "We've let 'em fuck us for too long." I think about Cora and whoever killed her. The Masons, and any other fuckers, over the years, that have taken advantage of our weakness.

"It ends. We find out who knocked up Breanna, we find out who killed Aubrey; and *you* grow a dick and make sure that woman you've loved your whole fuckin' life, doesn't marry into that bullshit family." I look at Wade sternly.

"It ain't that easy," he shakes his head.

"Nothin' worth having is fuckin' easy, Wade. Look at this place. It drove our grandpa to the fuckin' rope. But it's ours, and did you ever see a sunrise like that anywhere else?" I question, as I stare at the tall ridge behind the house that the sun is creeping over.

"He's gotta point," Cole backs me up. "It's too late to start throwin' fists in a fight when you've already lost. Don't leave it too late." I see the pain still raw in his eyes from losing Aubrey and have to look away.

"Looks like she showed up." Wade looks up ahead at the truck that's moving toward us, and when it pulls up in front of the gate and Maisie gets out, I hand Thunder's reins over to Cole and slide off his saddle.

"Hey." She smiles at me nervously, as I step toward her and take her hand.

"You sure about this?" I check, one last time.

"Don't just sit there staring, get back to the ranch. Finn, Dalton...get some shovels, ya goin' diggin'," I hear Mitch giving his order.

When Maisie nods her head back at me, I slowly lead her around the back of the horses, so she can see for herself why she never needs another sleepless night.

Her eyes take in the gruesome mess that's still left of Seth Granger, and the look on her face is unreadable. When he lets out another weak groan, reminding us all that he's still alive, her skin turns pale and she gags. Turning her body away from me she throws up in the grass.

"You ok?" I rub her back, trying to comfort her, worrying that this was a bad idea.

"I'm fine." She holds up her hand and catches her breath,

then turning back around, she keeps her eyes closed and draws a breath before looking at him again. There's something different in her expression now, something strong and wilful. Something accepting.

"You gotta gun?" She turns to look at me, and when I shake my head, she turns her attention to my brother.

"You...you gotta gun?" she stares at Cole, who flicks his eyes to me before he responds. When I nod, he rides his horse around to stand beside her, taking it from his holster and handing it down to her.

"Y'know how to use it?" he checks.

"Point and pull." She takes his revolver in her shaky hands and points it at Seth's head, pulling back the safety. Her eyes close tight, and her arms tremble as she holds it out in front of her. Just when I think she's about to drop it, her eyes open again, striking into his like a crack of lightning as she pulls back the trigger. The echo of the shot rings in the silence around us, and a crow calls out in the distance as we all stare at the dead man on the floor.

"Whatever it takes, right?" Maisie drops the gun on the floor before she turns to face me and my brothers. Using the back of her hand to wipe away the blood that's splattered on her cheek, she reaches up on her tiptoes and presses her lips against mine. "Thank you," she whispers, before stepping away and starting to walk back to the house.

"Oh..." she turns around, so she's walking backward. The smile on her face is just as pretty and innocent as the day I first saw her, "...you all be back at the house by eight thirty. We're having a family breakfast." She tugs on the sleeve of the off-shoulder sweater she's wearing, and spins back around.

"Sure thing, honey," I smile a little myself, as I call back to her. Ignoring the shocked look on Mitch and my brothers' faces, I hop back on Thunder.

"You married a psycho." Wade remains open mouthed as he watches her walking across the field toward the house.

"Here, help me load this son of a bitch into the back of the truck, we'll give them worms a warm meal for a change," Mitch sniggers at Wade as he unties the rope from the front of my saddle, and when Wade gets off Hooter and gets to work, Cole rides slowly back toward the house with me.

"You shouldn't have hid the fact you married her on my account," he tells me. This is the first time I've seen him since everyone found out. He's been sleeping in the bunkhouse, and he's yet to explain to me why.

"Yeah, well..."

"Well, nothin'. I'm your brother, all I ever want is for ya to be happy." He keeps facing forward, trying to hide the emotion in his eyes. "She's a good girl, stronger than we give her credit for."

"I'm learnin' that," I huff a laugh to myself; that girl never fails to surprise me.

"I'm gonna make it up to ya," he lets out a heavy breath.

"Make what up?" I question him, wondering what the hell he's talking about.

"Three years ago, I made a vow around that firepit, and I haven't been pulling my weight. I left you and Wade to pick up the slack around here, too, because I couldn't leave her. But I'm back now, and all that's changin'."

"Cole, ya don't need..."

"Will ya let me finish?" He stares at me in frustration. "I'm never gonna be the kinda uncle that Wade'll be to those kids you're havin'. I'm not gonna pick 'em up and ruffle their hair. I won't have the patience to teach 'em how to ride, or help 'em with their homework. But...I *can* make sure they get the time they deserve with their daddy. I *can* make sure that wife of yours doesn't end up wanting to divorce ya because you're never home in time for supper, and I *can* help you protect this place; so in thirty years' time they're teaching *their* kids how to rope up a calf in that corral. I ain't much of a brother, but I won't let ya down again." He grips his reins tight in his fist.

"You never let me down," I tell him, feeling a lump wedge in my throat. "And Carson men don't sleep in the bunkhouse. Ya belong with your family."

"Okay," Cole nods his head, and smiles.

"Now, you get in that house and give ya hot, psycho wife somethin' to smile about over breakfast." He tips his head toward the house, sniggering, and I click my tongue to get Thunder moving so I can do just that.

"Hey!" I've only got a few strides ahead when Cole calls out to me.

"'Bout that secret wedding of yours?"

"What about it?" I yell back.

"I'da been best man, right?"

"Sure," I laugh to myself, as I gallop all the way back to the yard.

I jump off Thunder's back, tossing the reins at the new ranch hand, before rushing indoors and calling out her name. I get no response, and when I hear the sound of running water coming from upstairs, I follow the sound to the bathroom.

Maisie's got her back to the glass, rinsing the shampoo out of her hair. I slowly creep up behind her, stripping out of my shirt, sliding slowly out of my boots, and pulling off my jeans.

She jumps when I step around the glass and grab that pretty, little face of hers in my hands, so I can kiss her.

"You shouldn't scare a pregnant woman like that," she pulls away, to tell me.

"There's plenty of things ya shouldn't do to a pregnant woman that I'm gonna," I warn her.

"So, can you still look me in the eye?" she stares up at me, curiously.

"What the hell ya talkin' about?" I shake my head, in confusion.

"I just shot a man right in front of you and your brothers. Do you still love me?" She's being deadly serious, and it makes my heart sink to think she'd ever doubt I couldn't.

"Of course I still fuckin' love ya, Maisie. There ain't nothin' in this whole world that could change that."

"So, why did you think it would change for *me?*" She's got that clever look on her face, and I press my palm against the glass behind her and drop my head when I understand the point she's making. "Do you doubt my feelings for you?"

"No, darlin', I don't." I lift my head back up.

"Good." She slides the wet hair, that's fallen over my eyes, to the side and brushes my cheek with her thumb.

"So, *you* just killed a man to prove a point?"

"No Garrett, I killed that man because he *deserved* to be dead. He tried to take something from me that I wasn't willing to give *and* he could have hurt our babies before they were even born. I shot that man in his head, and I felt no remorse. I feel no guilt now, only peace and I'd do it all over again to protect our family...but at the same time, it helped me prove a point," she smiles at me.

"You know, ya gonna fit in real good around here." I lift her up onto my body, letting my cock slide between her legs to tease her entrance.

"That's good, because I plan on sticking around," she whispers, gripping at my hair as I push inside her.

FIVE MONTHS LATER

I lie in bed and watch Maisie's huge stomach roll into all kinds of funny shapes.

"Which one was that?" I ask when something jolts, and she flinches.

"That will be your daughter, bossing her brothers around," she tells me, shifting up the bed into a more comfortable position.

"Well, in that case, you keep at it, sweetheart." I reach down and kiss her there, before getting out of bed and starting to get dressed.

"I thought I might do some more painting today to finish the piece Leia's dad wants for his office."

"I thought we agreed on ya takin' things easy?" I frown at her, as I button up my shirt.

"I'm not jumping on Darcy and entering a Kentucky Derby, Garrett. I'm painting," she huffs at me, before attempting to get out of bed herself.

"Yeah, I get that, but the doc said ya gotta start takin' it easy now. The longer you stay pregnant, the stronger the babies will be when they come," I remind her, as I step around the bed to help her up on her feet.

"They feel strong enough as it is." She takes a while to find her balance and looks up at me with a pout.

"Ya know what Doctor Handly said. One in five women carrying triplets ends up spendin' the last few weeks of their pregnancy in a hospital bed. D'ya wanna be that one in five?"

"No, that's not what I want," she lets out a disgruntled sigh, before waddling her way to the door to go to the bathroom.

"I'll bring ya easel and all ya supplies into the house so ya can work from here," I tell her, when she comes back a few minutes later.

"Ok, it's time to compromise." She grabs one of her dresses outta the wardrobe and stretches it over her body before letting me hear what this compromise is.

"Let me have one more day in the studio, and then I will do whatever you want until these babies come. I'll even let you hand feed me chocolate." She's got a sarcastic look on her face that makes me want to throw her on the bed and fuck the sass right out of her, but it's been advised we don't do that, either.

"Deal." I stroke my hands over her dress before kissing her goodbye and heading out to work.

It's past midday, and I'm fixing the rail on the corral that Wade crashed into with his new training project, this morning. Time's ticking on, Leia's wedding is getting closer, and he's still yet to do anything about it. Maisie's worried she won't be able to hang on long enough to be her matron of honor, and *I'm* hoping there won't be a wedding to hang on for. I've tried talking sense into him, but he seems in denial about the whole thing. I put it down to the fact he's scared, maybe he doesn't wanna put his heart on the line in case it gets broken, but he's only got five weeks left to decide if that fear is gonna be worth losing her.

The sun is shining bright for a March afternoon, and when I get a sense that I've seen all this before, my eyes automatically lift up to Maisie's studio door like they know what to expect. She's there just like I knew she would be, only this time it ain't a vision, it's real. My beautiful wife is standing beside her easel, her stomach swollen with our three babies growing inside it and she has the happiest smile on her face when she looks right back at me.

"Jesus Christ, ya really are goin' soft," Wade interrupts me, snatching the hammer outta my hand so he can take over.

"Go on, get up there and kiss her or somethin'." He shakes his head before getting to work, and that's exactly where I'm heading when I bump into Cole.

"What's up?" I stop in my tracks when I notice the look on his face.

"We expecting anyone?" I follow his line of vision back over my shoulder and notice the black, shiny car that's pulled up in front of the house.

"No." I shake my head, seeing that Wade has stopped what he's doing and is also paying attention. When the driver's door opens, and a smartly dressed woman gets out, I'm not prepared for what I see.

"You both look like you've seen a ghost." Maisie comes out of the hayloft and laughs. I take her hand in mine, bringing her close as I march toward our visitor, with my brothers at my flank.

Maybe this isn't reality; maybe this is just another dream because if what I'm seeing in front of me is for real, someone's gotta whole lot of explaining to do.

"Hey, boys." She smiles as she steps from behind her car door, and as she comes toward us, we all remain silent.

"I heard your news. Congratulations." She steps closer to Maisie, reaching out her hand like she's about to touch her stomach.

"Don't you *fuckin'* touch her!" I warn, snarling through my teeth, and when Maisie grips my hand a little tighter, I realize how confused she must be.

"Come on, Garrett, I raised you better than that. That's no way to welcome home your mother." The woman who abandoned us, nearly twenty years ago, smiles as if she never left.

Find out what happens with
Wade and Leia next-
TESTING LIMITS
Coming April 28, 2023

MORE FROM THE CORRUPT COWBOYS

1. OFF LIMITS
2. NO LIMITS

Start The Dirty Souls Series

0.5. **Bound Soul** (New Release Freebie)
1. **Lost Soul**
2. **Reckless Soul**
3. **Vengeful Soul**
4. **Damaged Soul**
5. **Forbidden Soul**
6. **Untamed Soul**
7. **Tortured Soul**
8. **Stolen Soul**
9. **Captivated Soul**
10. **Abandoned Soul**
11. **Ruined Soul**
(Coming April 2023)

ALSO BY EMMA CREED

STANDALONES

HIS CAPTIVE

HIS SACRIFICE

ABOUT THE AUTHOR

Come find/stalk me on the following social media platforms.

Printed in Great Britain
by Amazon

19629470R00140